ALSO BY
DARCY COATES

HOUSE
OF
SECRETS

DARCY COATES

Poisoned Pen
PRESS

Published by Poisoned Pen Press, an imprint of Sourcebooks
P.O. Box 4410, Naperville, Illinois 60567-4410
(630) 961-3900
sourcebooks.com

Originally self-published in 2016 by Black Owl Books.

Library of Congress Cataloging-in-Publication Data

Names: Coates, Darcy, author.
Title: House of secrets / Darcy Coates.
Description: Naperville, IL : Poisoned Pen Press, [2020] | "Originally
    self-published in 2016 by Black Owl Books"--Title page verso.
Identifiers: LCCN 2019056955 | (trade paperback)
Subjects: GSAFD: Ghost stories.
Classification: LCC PR9619.4.C628 H6896 2020 | DDC 823/.92--dc23
LC record available at https://lccn.loc.gov/2019056955

Printed and bound in the United States of America.
VP 11 10 9 8 7 6

CHAPTER 1
MOONLIT

SOPHIE WAS TRAPPED INSIDE the smothering red-and-gold hallways. The walls seemed to grow impossibly high to either side, and her breath plumed in the icy air as she scuttled away from the huge, dark shape that stalked her. It opened its vast black jaws, and ropes of saliva dropped onto the wood floor.

"No!" Sophie shrieked. Her back hit something solid, and she looked up. The red door was to her back, but its handle was far too high to reach.

Somewhere in the distance, Joseph screamed. He'd been torn open by the beast, and there was nothing she could do to save him. She couldn't even hold his hand and comfort him as he bled out.

The Grimlock reached its claws toward her face. Its maw stretched wide, and she could smell its fetid, rotting breath as it prepared to tear her in two.

Sophie screamed. The Grimlock's hands squeezed her, and she thrashed to pull free. But instead of feeling the sharp, cutting pain of teeth, Sophie realized she was struggling against something soft and giving. She opened her eyes and sucked in rapid, panicked breaths.

She was in her room. It was dark, but the coals in the fireplace still glowed, and the air was crisp, telling her it must be early morning.

She rolled onto her side to feel for Joseph's comforting warmth, but his half of the bed was empty. Dream and reality bled together for a second, and Sophie struggled to her feet, heart fluttering, as she prepared to search the labyrinthine Northwood for her husband.

No. Northwood was burned to the ground. It can't touch us any longer.

Sophie sank back onto the edge of her bed. The icy air sent chills through her as she gazed about the room.

She and Joseph had come directly to her father following their escape from Northwood, and they were staying at his city house until they could secure a property of their own. While the building wasn't tiny, it had a limited number of rooms, and Sophie and Joseph were sharing her old bedroom, which was still decorated in powder blue with bronze trimmings.

Sophie was glad to have her husband's company at night, but she couldn't stop the creeping worry that her feeling wasn't reciprocated. Every morning during the past week, she'd woken alone.

She tried to tell herself that Joseph was simply an early riser, but the sun hadn't yet breached the skyline, and when Sophie turned toward the window, she could make out a myriad of barely visible stars.

He's avoiding me. Sophie's hands were still shaking from the nightmare. She squeezed them together to keep them still and tried to slow her breathing. *But when we left Northwood two weeks ago, he loved me. I was so sure of it. I couldn't have misread his intentions, could I?*

"No." The word seemed to hover in the lonely room. *He told me he loved me. Once.*

Unable to sit any longer, Sophie rose and pulled her gown around her shoulders. The fireplace's glow was strong enough to show that Joseph's coat and hat no longer sat on the chair where he'd placed them the night before. That meant he'd gone out rather than simply moving to a different room in the house. Sophie crossed to the window and squinted at the ghostly shimmers of light that caught on the rooftops and cobblestones and hovered amid the fog. The street was undisturbed by man or beast.

It's not safe out at night. The only people still awake would slit Joseph's throat for his money.

Sophie squeezed her eyes closed and gripped the windowsill so tightly that her fingers ached. *No, he'll be safe. He's not foolish, and he can defend himself if it comes to that. But why did he go out so early? Did he have trouble sleeping, or did he want to be alone?*

A faint tapping made Sophie open her eyes. The sound came from the street below, but it echoed between the houses and made

Sophie unsure of its direction. Just as the noise resolved itself into brisk footsteps, a figure swept into view, its long legs gliding through the tendrils of mist. Sophie recognized the posture and quick pace as her husband's, and the band of anxiety around her chest loosened.

She turned from the window, intending to go downstairs and greet him at the door, but stopped herself. *He left so that he could be alone. Don't smother him; wait for him to come back to you.*

Sophie shed her gown and slid back into the bed. She listened to the downstairs door close with a muffled click, then she heard footsteps move through the foyer. She stayed awake for hours until the sun rose and dispelled the fog and the house was filled with the maids' footsteps and voices, but Joseph didn't rejoin her.

CHAPTER 2
BREAKFAST

SOPHIE SPENT LONGER THAN normal on dressing that morning. Joseph had once told her he liked her light-gold hair. She'd had her maid re-create a style she'd seen on a fashionable woman in town and weave tiny fake flowers through it. The style was more appropriate for an afternoon out than breakfast, but she didn't care about impressing the city's elite. She only wanted one man's notice.

By the time she hurried downstairs, the early-morning bustle had faded. Sophie's father, Mr. Hemlock, had left early for an appointment with his lawyer. Sophie was half-afraid that Joseph might have gone out too, but she found him in the breakfast room, reading the newspaper while he sipped tea.

"Good morning." Sophie moved toward the serving table and helped herself to cold meat and toast. "Did you sleep well?"

Joseph looked at her. Sophie felt a small spark of joy as his eyes flicked to her hair, but her triumph was crushed when he immediately returned his attention to the paper. "Yes, thank you."

"I'm glad." Sophie sat opposite her husband and furtively examined him. His pitch-black hair and dark eyes contrasted sharply with his pale skin. Sophie had always found his angled features deeply attractive, but his cheeks were a little too sunken for her to be happy about his health. The Grimlock, the creature that had inhabited their old home and had bound the Argenton family to its ancient bargain, had injured Joseph before they'd escaped. The only remnants of that battle were a myriad of ice-white scars across his torso and a lingering gauntness. *He's still healing*, she reminded herself. *Uncle Phillip has been treating him, and there's no one I would trust more to care for Joseph.*

Sophie picked at her food as she struggled to find a way to break the silence. "Is there any interesting news?"

Again, she earned herself a brief glance before he returned to the paper. "Not today. A theft. Scandals. A fire that was contained before it could spread. Nothing that affects us."

"Well…I suppose I prefer dull news to bad news."

This time Joseph's eyes met hers and stayed there. A smile flickered over his lips. "Yes, I suppose I do too." He didn't speak for a moment before murmuring, so quietly that Sophie wasn't sure she was supposed to have heard, "You look beautiful."

Sophie couldn't stop the heat from spreading over her face. She beamed and knotted her hands in the folds of her dress as her heart jumped. His smile, his words, the warmth in his eyes—she felt as though she'd been transported back to the days following the Grimlock's defeat, when Joseph's affection had been unguarded and generous. "I—"

A door above them slammed, followed by a shriek of laughter from Sophie's younger brother and a hushed scolding from the governess. The noise intruded like a knife cutting them apart, and Joseph turned to his newspaper with the same indifferent expression he'd worn when she'd entered the room. Their brief moment might as well have not existed.

Sophie tried to swallow the disappointment as she returned to picking at her breakfast. *Is there something wrong with him? Have I made him unhappy? Or is it this house? I can't imagine him wanting to live with my family for much longer. Yet he still hasn't raised the subject of moving. Has he already started looking for a suitable property, or would he tell me first?*

As Sophie examined the man opposite her, she was struck with the unsettling sensation that she was watching a stranger. They'd been married for barely three weeks, and most of their first days as husband and wife had been muddied with secrets and lies. Following Northwood's destruction, they'd shared a brief euphoric period when Joseph had kissed her eagerly and kept her awake late into the night. But within days of their return to her father's house, his attentions had stopped.

She'd spun through every excuse she could find. *He's not used to the bustle of the city, and it's exhausted him; he's recovering from his injuries; he's still coming to terms with the change in circumstances; he's grieving his aunt's death; he misses his uncle and cousin.*

But as the days passed and Joseph showed no symptoms of

stress, pain, or loneliness, Sophie had been forced to turn to more distressing options: the source of his discontent was either their house…or her.

You were a fool to think he would love you, a cruel little voice whispered in the back of her mind. *It was a loveless marriage; what did you expect the result to be—that you would defy the odds and find a partner who would reciprocate your feelings? Stop being naïve. He needed a wife to sacrifice to the Grimlock. He chose you on a whim. And now that he's free from the beast, he's begun to regret his decision.*

"Have you thought about where we should move?" The words escaped her in a desperate rush, and her insides turned cold from embarrassment. Sophie hadn't intended to speak so brashly or quickly.

Joseph looked up. "I'm pleased to stay here as long as your father welcomes us."

"Oh." Sophie tried to place her cutlery on the plate but released the fork too soon and grimaced at the sharp clatter. She cleared her throat. "I thought…I…"

Joseph folded the paper and set it to one side. He clasped his hands on the table and leaned forward so that Sophie couldn't avoid his gaze. Although the force of his attention was unnerving, his voice was soft. "Go on."

"It might be nice…to be established in our own house…"

Joseph let the silence stretch until Sophie began to worry she'd made the situation worse. Then he said with no discernible emotion, "If you like."

Is he annoyed? Did I speak out of turn?

Sophie opened her mouth, floundering for some words to ease the tension, but was spared having to speak when the housekeeper entered the room in a bustle of thick skirts. "Begging your pardons, but a letter has arrived for Mr. Argenton. Express."

Joseph's eyebrows drew together as he held out his hand for the note. The housekeeper passed it to him, bobbed a curtsy, and left. Joseph was silent as he broke the letter open and read.

Sophie tried to guess his thoughts. They clearly weren't pleasant. His expression hardened, his lips tightening and his brow lowering until he was glowering at the paper. A strange intensity entered his eyes. Not for the first time, he reminded Sophie of a wild animal barely contained behind a veneer of civility.

She couldn't read the contents, but she could see that the note was short. Joseph read it twice before dropping it to the table and lacing his hands under his chin.

"Well, my dear," he said at last. His voice, raw and cold, sent chills through Sophie. "It seems we will not escape today without bad news after all."

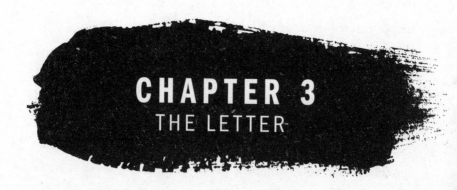

CHAPTER 3
THE LETTER

JOSEPH NODDED TOWARD THE note. "Read it. You deserve to know."

Sophie hated the hard tone of his voice. She reached for the paper with cold hands and smoothed it out. Even though the writer didn't have an even hand, the message had clearly been formed with care. Every new line brought a different emotion to Sophie—shock, then horror, then dread—thick and cloistering and freezing the air in her lungs.

Joseph,

It's not dead.

The Grimlock escaped Northwood's burning. It has attached itself to Elise. We have retreated to the Kensington property, where I request your immediate assistance.

Forgive me.

Garrett

At the base of the letter was an address.

"No…" Sophie murmured. "It can't be possible."

She looked at Joseph and saw the grim lines marring his face. He clearly didn't doubt the letter's contents. Despairing, she dropped her gaze back to the note and searched through her memories of their last night at Northwood. It had been full of fire and smoke and the screams of those long dead. She'd been frantic, and the images bled together like those in a dream, but she recalled the Grimlock in detail, its oily black flesh scorched by the flames, its eyes rolling madly in its skull as it staggered through the building. She'd instinctively known that it was near death. Northwood had not only been its home but also its heart—the place that anchored it to the human realm—and the manor's destruction should have caused the beast's death.

"It has attached itself to Elise."

Sophie remembered how Rose, loyal to the Grimlock, had thrown herself at its feet and pledged her aid. In response, the Grimlock had attacked and eaten her.

It was starving that night; Rose was the first victim it had consumed in years. How much energy did it gain? Enough to transfer its anchor to a new vessel?

Then she remembered sitting on the grass with Joseph, Garrett, and Elise as they watched Northwood burn. She'd been too worried for Joseph to pay her other companions much attention, but she'd noticed a dazed look in Elise's eyes. She'd assumed the girl was in shock. What if it had been something far worse, and none of them had identified the symptoms?

"It's not dead."

Sophie raised her head to see Joseph watching her. A cold ferocity smoldered in his eyes, and his jaw was set. She didn't want to ask if he was going because she already knew the answer. Joseph would travel to his family and fight the Grimlock. And he would die.

Her throat tightened. A distorted, high-pitched ringing filled her ears, cutting off rational thought, and tears burned at her eyes. Sophie pushed away from the table and turned toward the door.

"Sophie."

Joseph's bark turned her walk into a run. She couldn't stand to sit with him and discuss the inevitable. She needed time to think. Sophie took the stairs two at a time and followed the hallway toward her bedchamber. She pushed the door closed behind her and rested her back against the wood. No footsteps followed.

She made herself draw several long breaths then wiped the wetness off her cheeks. The room felt bizarrely calm compared to the turmoil scraping at her insides. She crossed to the window and leaned against it, her eyes roving across the milling crowds and coaches below as she tried to arrange her thoughts.

She hadn't heard of Kensington before, which meant it was at least several days' travel by coach. Joseph would respond to

Garrett's request. That much was certain; he was loyal to his family and wouldn't ignore their suffering. And even if Sophie managed to convince him to stay—whether by begging, tears, or some combination of the two—he would never forgive her for it. She had to consider Joseph's actions as outside her control, but the other half of the equation—what happened once Joseph arrived at Kensington—was still alterable.

At Northwood, the Grimlock had been restricted to living behind the red door, which opened into a mirror version of the mansion. Sophie was still unsure exactly where or how that mirror Northwood had existed, but she'd read a phrase in a book that seemed surprisingly apt: other dimension.

In the mirror house, the Grimlock had been a tall, inky-black, naked beast with claws longer than Sophie's forearm and hollow lights instead of eyes. Now that Northwood was destroyed and the creature had latched itself onto Elise, Sophie didn't know what to expect. Would it be an intangible force controlling the girl—who had always been susceptible to its influence—or would it still retain its physical shape? *Why couldn't Garrett have been more detailed in his letter?*

Sophie turned and paced the room as she chewed on the corner of her thumb. As horrified as she was to think of Elise being manipulated by the monster, she feared its physical manifestation far more. The Grimlock was strong, fast, and intelligent. Sophie also suspected it held grudges, which would explain why the Grimlock had latched onto Elise rather than one of the house's servants.

It will try to kill Joseph. Another memory came, this one unbidden and far more horrible than any of the previous: Joseph, lying on the mirror Northwood's tiled foyer, his limbs twitching as the Grimlock tore flesh from his torso.

Sophie pressed her hand over her mouth as nausea rose. *He's not dead. The bleeding stopped as soon as he was carried through the red door. Don't dwell on it; we were able to rescue him.*

Sophie dropped her hand and raised her head to blink away the tears. *I saved him last time—I set Northwood on fire, stayed with him while the building filled with flames, and helped Garrett carry him outside. Maybe if I go to Kensington with him...*

She took a deep, slow breath and laced her hands together as a grim hope built inside of her. *At the very least, we'd be together even if it meant death for both of us.*

It was pure insanity to return to the Grimlock, but the idea of losing her husband was far more abhorrent. The tall, black-eyed stranger had become dear to her during her stay at Northwood, and the thought of him dying alone and at the Grimlock's mercy made her shake. *If I were with him, though—if I could help a little, watch over him, and maybe even protect him...*

Sophie turned to her wardrobe, threw the doors open, and began pulling out clothing.

CHAPTER 4
GOODBYES

SOPHIE'S TRAVEL CASE WAS nearly packed when Joseph entered their bedroom. Sophie resisted the temptation to turn around and instead focused on folding a coat.

When she'd moved to Northwood, she'd packed clothes the mistress of a great estate would be expected to wear. This time, however, she only cared about practicality. Which dresses could she run in? What clothing would keep her warm if they weren't able to light a fire? What was comfortable enough to sleep in?

Joseph didn't speak but stood in the doorway as he watched her. Sophie, unnerved by his silence, licked her lips and tried to keep her voice light. "How soon will we leave?"

"We?" There was a smile in Joseph's voice. Sophie gave in to the temptation and turned to face him. The tall man watched her keenly, his arms folded and eyebrows raised. "*I* shall depart at first light. *You* will stay with your father."

Sophie had been expecting resistance. She returned to the luggage and hoped her voice sounded calmer than she felt. "The Grimlock's return is as much my concern as it is yours. I helped destroy Northwood, and I can help again now."

A warm hand stroked the hair away from the back of her neck, and Sophie shivered. Joseph had approached her so carefully that she hadn't even heard his footsteps. "You're a brave woman. But I will not allow you to fight my battles. Your involvement at Northwood was unavoidable and something that I severely regret. And it is also a very strong argument for your staying here."

Sophie frowned. "I don't understand."

"*You* were responsible for the destruction of the Grimlock's home. *You* nearly killed it. The Grimlock is no longer indifferent to you, my dear, which means bringing you to Kensington goes beyond simple endangerment; it would be offering a dove to a lion."

Sophie rotated. Joseph stood so close that she could feel the warmth from his chest. She wanted to touch him—to wrap her arms around him and relax into the safety and comfort his presence gave her—but knotted her fingers together instead. "I will be in less danger than you. Yes, I dealt the final blow, but you, Garrett, and Elise had been fighting the Grimlock for decades. If you hadn't gone through the red door to challenge it, I wouldn't have followed. The Grimlock may hate me, but its anger will be directed at the Argentons."

A smile tugged at Joseph's mouth. "You are *also* an Argenton now."

"I-I meant—"

"I know." His fingers, exquisitely gentle, brushed a strand of hair away from her face. "I admire your willingness—even your enthusiasm—to accompany me. But you are to stay here. It is not a matter I wish to discuss any further."

Sophie didn't know where to look or what to say. Frustration and fear tangled inside her, but Joseph's tone had been so final that she suspected her arguments would harm more than help.

Joseph's hand lingered on her neck where he'd brushed the hair away. Warmth spread from the connection, and Sophie leaned into the touch. Before she knew what was happening, Joseph's lips were on hers, his spare hand tangling in her hair. The kiss promised all of the love and desire that Sophie had been starving for. She melted into him, eager and pliant, as he tugged her closer. Then Joseph pulled back with a gasp and stepped away.

"Your father was asking for you." His voice held an edge of rawness, but the shutters had returned to his eyes. He nodded toward the door. "I have already explained to him that I will be traveling and do not know when I will return."

Sophie opened her mouth, but Joseph had already turned and swept out of the room. She realized she still had her hands raised as though to clutch at him and prevent him from leaving, and she lowered them. Her mind buzzed. The kiss had been everything she'd wanted, but Joseph had broken it off so quickly and followed it with such dispassionate words that she was left even more confused than before.

He didn't mean it, the cynical voice at the back of her mind whispered. *He only kissed you because he was tired of arguing and knew it would silence your objections. And look—it worked.*

"Quiet," Sophie hissed and strode out of the room. The house's air tasted stuffy, and she struggled to breathe as she hurried to the ground floor. The two sides of her mind argued during the entire walk, and she wasn't conscious of where her feet were carrying her until she looked up and found herself in front of the door to her father's study.

Sophie closed her eyes to calm her fragmented mind. When she touched her hair, she found the careful arrangement had been mussed by Joseph's attentions. She flushed and tucked the loose strands back into a respectable order before knocking on the old wooden door.

"Come in." Mr. Hemlock sat behind his desk but rose as Sophie entered. "Ah, my dear."

Sophie managed a smile. The room was airy, warm—thanks to its fire—and decorated with dark wood and plush chaise longues. She took the seat her father indicated and waited as he sat next to her. "Is everything all right?"

"I was hoping you could answer that." Mr. Hemlock laced his fingers under his chin as he examined her. To Sophie's eyes, he'd aged remarkably since she'd married Joseph. The wrinkles about his brow were more set and his gray hair a shade lighter, but the creases about his mouth, built up by a lifetime of smiles, were as strong as ever. "Your husband just told me that he was leaving and had little intention of coming back."

Sophie hesitated then spoke carefully. "Did he explain why?"

She and Joseph had conferred about how much of their experience to share when they returned to society. They'd decided to say an unnamed servant forgot to extinguish a fire one night, and Northwood had been burned to the ground. At the time, there had been nothing to be gained by trying to convince their peers of the existence of a dark, malevolent monster.

Mr. Hemlock frowned. "No. And—forgive me for saying this—he's not the sort of man I would want to impose too many questions on. I was hoping you would tell me."

Sophie inhaled but didn't have any words to breathe life into. She wished she could avoid her father's scrutiny; she hated seeing worry and sadness etched in his face.

"Did you argue?" Mr. Hemlock asked. "My dear, don't think you are the first couple to have a spat. Breaches can be repaired—"

"No, nothing like that." Sophie twisted her hands in her lap. She wanted her father to know what was happening but couldn't tell him about the Grimlock without raising a thousand difficult questions. Then an idea, a half lie that would let her share her worries without causing alarm, occurred to her. "Joseph intends to duel an old enemy."

Mr. Hemlock's eyebrows rose. "Ah."

"And—and his opponent is an excellent marksman—"

"I see. And you fear your husband won't return."

Sophie's throat had tightened too much to speak. She nodded.

Mr. Hemlock leaned forward in his chair. "Dueling is a foolish sport that rarely fixes wrongs and often wastes a great deal of potential. Is it something you can convince him to give up?

Your uncle and I will gladly add our voices; I know Mr. Argenton holds a great deal of respect for your uncle."

Sophie shook her head again. She tried to speak clearly, though a quiet panic was choking her. "Thank you. But he is determined. It is…a very old grievance and one that the other party is pursuing more than Joseph. There is no way to dissuade him."

Mr. Hemlock sighed and held a hand toward her. "I'm deeply sorry, my dear."

Sophie took the hand and let herself be pulled into a hug. She buried her face against her father's shoulder and squeezed her eyes closed as he patted the back of her head.

"I understand this is painful, my dear," Mr. Hemlock murmured. "But if it must happen, at least it is early in your marriage and before too much attachment can develop. And think: in case of the worst outcome, you're still young enough to remarry if you wish."

A cold horror twisted through Sophie's chest. She knew her father meant the words as comfort, but they made her want to scream. She pulled out of his embrace and managed a thin smile. "I-I'm not feeling well. If you'll excuse me, I'd like to retire early."

Mr. Hemlock sighed. "Of course. Poor child; of course this is very distressing for you. Should I ask the maid to bring you some warm milk?"

"Thank you, but I just need rest."

Mr. Hemlock squeezed her hand then waved her toward the door. "Good night, my dear."

"Goodbye," Sophie replied. Her dry eyes ached as she climbed the stairs and entered her room. The travel case still stood on the bed, waiting to be unpacked. Sophie regarded it for a moment then carefully placed the final cloak inside, closed the lid, and slid it under the bed.

CHAPTER 5
THE SECOND COACH

SOPHIE READ HER LETTER a final time. It was short, but she hoped it managed to express all of the gratitude and affection that she felt for her family without sounding like a final goodbye.

That was its purpose, of course—not just to explain why she'd left with Joseph but also to provide comfort in the event that she didn't return. It hadn't been an easy balance; a dozen prior versions had been turned to ash in the fireplace.

Her bedroom door opened, and Sophie slipped the note into the desk's drawer before turning to face Joseph.

He looked exhausted. "Your father said you weren't feeling well."

"I'm fine now, thank you." Sophie rose and went to him, but he made no move to kiss her. She tried not to let the disappointment show. "I—is there anything I can help with—"

Joseph folded his coat over the back of the chair beside the door. "Thank you, but everything is prepared. I spoke to my accountant. If I don't return inside of three weeks, he will arrange for my assets to be released to you. They will provide a comfortable living for you for the remainder of your life."

He talks as though his death is certain.

Joseph crossed to the desk and placed his hat and a letter on its edge. His voice was disturbingly calm. "Please don't feel you have any obligation to remain loyal to me. If you wish to remarry after the mourning period—"

"Don't say that," Sophie said, choking on the words. The cold dread was rising inside of her again. She moved to Joseph's side and took his hand. "You're strong. You'll return."

Joseph didn't respond. Sophie searched his eyes but couldn't find any trace of fear. Instead, a deep sadness saturated them, and the expression frightened her even more than his silence. She tightened her grip. "You can't have given up all hope. W-we don't know what to expect at Kensington. The Grimlock could be vulnerable a-and weak."

The sadness dissolved into a wry smile, and Joseph's hand rose to caress her cheek. "I didn't mean to distress you. Don't worry for me, my dear. Of course, I fully intend to return if possible." The fingers moved past her jaw and down her throat to tease at the dress's neckline. The touch sent heat rushing into her face. "It's late, and I will have to leave early tomorrow. Are you ready to come to bed?"

Later that night, Sophie lay on her side, watching Joseph breathe. His face was relaxed and black hair ruffled. One of his arms draped across Sophie's waist, a remnant of their earlier embrace. They'd been intimate for the first time since returning home. Joseph's intensity had thrilled Sophie but also frightened her. It had felt like a goodbye.

Moonlight fell through the curtained window and scattered shadows across their room. Sophie felt exhausted, but a combination of adrenaline and anxiety kept her awake. She was grateful for that; there was an important task to complete before she could sleep.

When she judged Joseph's slumber deep enough, Sophie carefully squirmed away from him. The loss of his touch made her feel cold, but he didn't stir as Sophie slipped out of bed and pulled her nightgown on.

She padded toward the desk and collected the letter from under Joseph's hat. As she'd hoped, it was Garrett's note. The writing was too small to read by moonlight, so Sophie took a candle from the desk and lit it in the fireplace's embers. She glanced back at Joseph as the wick flickered to life. He remained still.

Back at the desk, Sophie pulled out a clean sheet of paper. Garrett had included Kensington's address below his message, and Sophie copied it. She gave the paper a quick wave to dry the ink then slid it into the drawer beside her letter to her family.

She turned back to her bed and gasped. Although Joseph remained still, his eyes were open, and the candle's light reflected off the black irises.

When did he wake? Did he see me take Garrett's note? "I-I—"

"Couldn't you sleep, my dear?" Joseph's voice was low but

surprisingly gentle. Sophie shook her head, and he finally shifted to stretch his hand toward her. "Come back to bed. I want to be near you tonight."

Sophie's heart thundered so loudly that she was sure he would hear it, but there was no recrimination in his face as he gently pulled her back under the sheets. She settled at his side and relaxed as he pressed a kiss against her forehead. "Sleep, my dear," he whispered.

She intended to stay awake through the night, but Joseph caressed her back until the tension fled and tiredness rolled in to take its place. She fell into a fitful, disjointed sleep.

It was still dark when she woke. Joseph had disappeared from her side, and the room was quiet and empty. She turned over and saw the fire had been revived, though, which meant he couldn't have been gone for more than an hour.

Sophie stumbled out of bed, too anxious to move carefully but still too sleepy to be coordinated. She struggled into her traveling clothes and pulled the packed case out from under her bed.

"Slow down," Sophie told herself as she lifted the case onto the bed. "There's no use in rushing."

She planned to travel to Kensington in Joseph's wake. If the journey was as long as she anticipated, he'd have a difficult time turning her away when she arrived. He'd be angry, but she'd rather face his displeasure than spend the next month at home, listening to every carriage that passed their door and praying that one would contain her husband.

Sophie went to fetch the address from the drawer and felt

her heart skip a beat when she found it gone. *He saw me copy it after all.* The letter she'd written to her family remained, but Kensington's address had been destroyed—burned in the fire most likely.

Sophie closed her eyes and inhaled deeply. Joseph might have removed the physical directions, but he couldn't erase her memories. She could still picture the address written out in Garrett's scratchy scrawl.

She took her own letter from the drawer and placed it in the center of the desk, where it couldn't be missed. She then took her case and crept out of her room and down the stairs, keeping to their edges. The travel case was heavy, but she didn't dare ask one of the footmen for help. If the staff realized she was running away, they would wake Mr. Hemlock, and Sophie wanted to be a good distance from home before her father was alerted to her absence.

Her breath plumed in the icy air as she struggled down the street, fighting to keep her footsteps light without dropping the case. Her boots were loud against the cobblestones, and the noise echoed between the tightly packed houses. Sophie prayed no one from her house would hear or, if they did, they wouldn't look through the windows.

She'd sent a request for a coach the day before, asking them to wait for her around the corner, out of sight of her father's home, and to be ready to pick her up between four and six in the morning. She turned the corner and felt relief spark through her at the sight of the dark carriage. The coachman climbed down and took her luggage. Sophie quickly told him the address. "Can you take me there?"

The wiry man squinted at her and scratched his stubbled chin. "It's five days' travel. I can get you as far as Bromson, and post will take you most of the rest."

"Good." Sophie let the coachman help her into the carriage and released her breath as he closed the door behind her.

Joseph would have a few hours' head start on her. She needed to put some distance between herself and her home before her family realized she was missing, but then she intended to lengthen Joseph's lead to half a day by asking her coach to wait a little longer the first time they changed horses. It was a difficult balance—if she traveled too fast and accidentally caught up to Joseph, he would send her home. But she didn't want to allow too much of a gap either. A lot could happen in half a day.

She expected Joseph to move quickly. He wouldn't sleep more than a few hours each night, if at all, and wouldn't stop any more frequently than he had to. Once she had the half-day buffer between them and there was no risk of stopping at the same inn at the same time, Sophie intended to match his pace. Ideally, they would arrive at Kensington on the same day.

Be safe until then, Sophie prayed as she watched the sunrise bleach the sky above the city's rooftops. *Don't do anything risky.*

The coach was able to make good time while the streets were near empty, and by the time the sun had risen and melted the frost from the grass, she had escaped the city and was traveling through the countryside.

Sophie felt dazed. The discovery of the Grimlock's survival, the idea of losing Joseph, and the decision to follow him had all happened so quickly that the previous day seemed like a dream. She regretted not being able to say a proper goodbye to her family—especially her siblings, who were too young to fully understand. But when she searched her conscience, she felt she'd made the right decision.

Despite the gnawing anxiety, she couldn't stop herself from pressing against the window to watch the passing landscape. Huge oak and elm trees grew along the side of the road, and a little farther, past the farmland, were deep forests. She loved the countryside and wondered if Joseph would prefer living on a rural property or staying in town.

It was another bitter reminder of how little she knew about the man she'd married. *Can you even call it love when the feelings are for a stranger?* the cold inner voice asked. Sophie pushed it to the back of her mind.

They stopped at an inn a little before lunch. Sophie guessed Joseph would have changed horses and traveled on without resting. She asked her coach's attendant to wait while she ate and passed him an extra coin for his own meal before entering the inn and requesting a room.

The inn's maid was eager to please and happy to answer Sophie's questions. Yes, a tall, black-haired gentleman had stopped there barely three hours before. She'd brought him some water. Yes, he'd moved on immediately. Yes, he'd looked in good health, as well as she could judge.

Sophie thanked the girl and settled down to wait. The food was fresh and generous, but she struggled to eat. She wanted to leave at least six hours between their carriages in case Joseph was laid over for any reason, but nervous energy and impatience got the better of her, and she returned to her coach after an hour.

More countryside lay ahead of them. Sophie hadn't had time to locate Kensington on a map, but they seemed to be moving into increasingly untamed landscapes. The farmland was gradually giving way to empty fields and rolling hills. By late afternoon, her legs were aching from being constrained in the carriage, and she was tempted to ask the attendant to stop so that she could take a walk. The light was beginning to fade, though, and she thought she could see a faint glow in a valley below them, which she guessed would be the town they were to stop at.

She was right. They descended a slope that was too steep for the horses to handle comfortably, then the road opened into a small village. Sophie thought there couldn't be more than a hundred houses scattered about the area, and the stores they passed were small and shabby.

The coach came to a halt outside the only inn in sight, and her door was pulled open. She took the hand that was offered to her, stepped out of the coach, then drew back with a horrified gasp.

"Well, my dear," Joseph said, refusing to release her hand. "I wish I could say I was surprised."

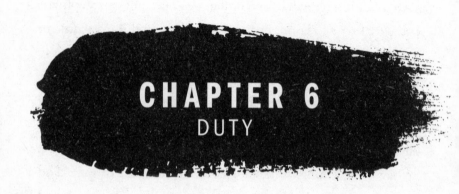

CHAPTER 6
DUTY

SOPHIE'S MIND WENT BLANK. She impulsively tried to step back inside the coach, but Joseph didn't loosen his grip. Instead, he pulled her nearer, his dark eyes scanning her face. "This is incredibly inconvenient."

"I-I'm sorry—"

Joseph watched her face for a long moment, then he sighed, and his expression softened. "You look tired. Come inside; we'll have some food and see if we can decide on a reasonable solution."

Sophie allowed her husband to thread her arm through his and followed him into the inn. He led her to a private room, settled her at one side of the table, and sat opposite. Sophie couldn't bring herself to meet his eyes. Embarrassment heated her face and stuck her throat closed, but she clung to her resolution like a drowning man to a plank.

Joseph let the silence stretch for a moment then nodded toward the food laid out before them. "Eat something."

"I'm not hungry, thank you." That was true; her appetite had vanished.

"Then we'll have some tea instead." Joseph rose, went to the door to pass his request on to the maid, then folded his arms and leaned against the doorframe.

Sophie waited for him to speak, but he remained silent. When she searched for frustration or anger in his face, she was unnerved by how passive his expression was. *He looks tired. No, more than that...tired and sad. Because of me?*

The maid entered with their tea. Joseph waited until she'd left the room before pouring two cups and passing one to Sophie. Instead of settling back at his place opposite her, he rounded the table and drew up a seat at her side. One hand brushed a lock of her hair behind her ear, and Sophie inhaled at the touch.

"You cannot come to Kensington with me." Joseph's voice was soft but firm. "You *must* understand this."

Sophie clenched her fists to stop them from trembling. She still couldn't meet his eyes. "I have as much right as you do."

"No. This is my duty—my curse—in the same way that it's my duty to ensure your safety."

Sophie fought to keep the frown off her face. She searched for a good rebuttal, but her mind failed her.

Joseph sighed. "You've put me in a difficult situation. Time is of the essence, and now I will need to escort you home. Mercy knows I can't trust you to complete the journey yourself."

This time his voice held a bite of annoyance. Sophie straightened her back and stared at the bread on the table as though it would lend her strength. "Save yourself the time. Even if you return me, I'll come back. I've memorized the address."

A flash in Joseph's eyes told her she was entering dangerous territory. "Then I'll have your father lock you in your room."

She raised her chin and prayed her voice would be steady. "I'll escape."

Joseph hissed and pushed away from the table. He thrust his hands into his pockets and stalked across the room, pausing beside the fire before turning. His stance was threatening, but his expression gave Sophie a flicker of hope. He looked cornered... almost panicky. "Why are you so intent on following? Do you imagine it will fix anything?"

They were skirting the subject Sophie had been terrified of raising. Joseph seemed to be a second away from saying *Do you think it will make me love you again?* But the words never left his lips.

"No," Sophie said carefully, every nerve buzzing, her heart aching from the iron squeeze of anxiety. "I believe it will make me happy."

She wanted to say more—to tell him that she wasn't asking him for his love, only for the chance to win it—but her tongue wouldn't form the words. Joseph watched her, rubbed the back of his hand across his mouth, and paced the length of the room twice.

"I know you're smart," he said at last. "And brave. Caring.

Conscientious. But I didn't expect you to be this *stubborn*." He scowled at her, but something told Sophie the expression was an act. "Most women simply obey their husbands' wishes."

"Most women don't have husbands running into mortal peril."

Joseph's brows rose, then he chuckled, and the tension in Sophie's chest eased. He moved back to the table and sat beside her, folding his long legs ahead of himself and crossing his arms. He stared at the ceiling for a long stretch. The only noise was the fire's crackle and the distant, echoing voices of the inn's other occupants. Then he spoke carefully. "Very well. Come to Kensington if you feel you must—but on one condition."

Sophie nodded, waiting for the terms.

"As you said, we don't know what to expect from the Grimlock. My uncle wouldn't have summoned me if it were a hopeless case. But that doesn't mean it's safe. If we arrive and the situation is too dangerous for you to linger, you will return home immediately. Do you agree?"

"Yes," Sophie said without hesitation. She didn't intend to leave his side under any circumstances, but that was a battle she would fight when she needed to. For the moment, having Joseph's permission to accompany him was enough of a victory.

"You had better eat something, then. I intend to leave within a half hour and travel through the night. I hope you don't mind sleeping in the carriage."

"Of course not." Sophie pulled a plate toward herself. She scanned the dishes and saw that they hadn't been touched, so she served Joseph as well as herself. He didn't object. As she cut into the duck, Sophie murmured, "It will be nice to have some company for the trip."

"Yes," Joseph said, his voice soft as he picked at the bread. "I suppose it will."

CHAPTER 7
THE DEAD TOWN

SOPHIE, EAGER TO PROVE she wouldn't be a hindrance, ate quickly and was ready to leave within ten minutes. Joseph's carriage was larger than the one she'd taken, but the addition of a traveling companion and his luggage meant there was less room. They sat side by side, shoulders bumping, but rarely speaking, and watched the changing landscape through their windows.

As evening turned to night, Sophie tried to sleep against the door. The constant rolling motion was almost hypnotic, but it also jolted her awake whenever she drew near slumber. Each time she woke, she glanced toward Joseph. Usually he was looking through his window, watching the black trees' silhouettes shift past, but once she caught him watching her. He beckoned. "Here, lean on me."

Sophie rested her head against his shoulder. It was easier to sleep like that, and she only woke once more, near early morning, to find the chilly air had invaded their carriage and Joseph had draped his coat over her.

Morning came at last and with it a stop at an inn to change horses. They ate a quick breakfast, and Sophie washed her face and arms, changed clothes, and did what she could to make her hair respectable. Then it was back into the carriage for another day of traveling.

Sophie hadn't expected the trip to be so grueling. The only two long journeys she'd taken before—one to Northwood and one returning home—had been interspersed with nights spent at inns and leisurely stops for each meal. She felt sore from constantly sitting, and the motion, which had become worse since they'd left the smooth town roads behind, made her feel vaguely sick. Joseph looked pale too. She didn't know whether he'd slept the night before, only that he'd been awake and alert each time she'd woken.

"Tell me about Kensington," she said shortly after they changed horses at noon. "I haven't heard of it before."

"It used to be a grand house before it was abandoned." Joseph kept his attention on the passing scenery, but he seemed happy to talk. "It belonged to the Bishop family, who were a distant branch of the royal family. The Bishop lineage ultimately resolved to two siblings: a gentleman, Thomas, and his sister, Madeleine. Thomas Bishop had the poor fortune of meeting a Miss Anne Argenton during one of his visits to town. He fell in love and asked for her hand in marriage."

"Oh."

"I see you can guess the outcome of that liaison. Mr. Bishop most likely intended to bring his wife back to Kensington, but once they were married, he was pulled into the Argenton curse and bound to Northwood. That was during one of my family's more prosperous eras, and I understand he lived a long life before being taken by the Grimlock."

Sophie felt a stab of pity for the man. He wouldn't have known about the Grimlock before his marriage, but once bound to the family, there was no escape save death.

"Kensington legally belonged to Mr. Bishop, but because he wasn't able to live in it, he let Madeleine stay there as a way to provide for her. She never married and had no heirs, so on her death a little over a hundred years ago, the property's title reverted to my family. It has sat empty ever since."

"And that's why Garrett moved there," Sophie said. "So that he wouldn't need to waste time finding a building to lease."

"Truthfully, Kensington isn't an isolated situation. A number of estates—some very wealthy—married into the Argenton family and had their property revert to our ownership upon their demise. We have empty buildings scattered across the country. Many are so dilapidated that it would cost more to repair them to a livable state than we would earn from their sale, so they have been allowed to lie dormant."

Sophie frowned. She'd known her husband was wealthy, but she still hadn't expected him to own multiple properties. "Is there a reason he chose Kensington?"

"I can't speak on his behalf, but I have my suspicions. First,

Garrett would not want the risk of strangers calling to welcome him to the neighborhood while the Grimlock lives with him. Kensington overlooks a town, but the area relied on the estate to remain prosperous, and families began to move away when Thomas Bishop left for Northwood. I believe a handful clung on until Miss Bishop's death, but the settlement is now a ghost town."

Sophie wanted to blame her shiver on the cold air. Joseph's hand brushed her neck, checking her temperature, then he bent forward and pulled a spare coat from his travel case. He wrapped it about Sophie before settling back.

"The second reason for Garrett's choice is far more intriguing. There are rumors of letters, written by Miss Bishop and delivered to her brother, in which she claimed to be researching ways to dispel the Grimlock. I suspect Garrett hopes to find some help at Kensington. Madeleine Bishop apparently passed away before she found a solution, but it's possible there will be research notes, books, or other sources of information."

Sophie remembered the volume her father had accidentally bought from a peddler when she was a child: *Cryptids and the Occult*, a book dedicated to ghosts, monsters, and moving shadows. It had given her nightmares as a child, but the vague memory of an entry on the Grimlock had provided Sophie with the knowledge she needed to fight the monster. She wondered if Miss Bishop might have found the same book. She dearly wanted to reread the passages.

Joseph shifted and frowned. "Can you tolerate this carriage

for one more night, my dear? The journey would normally take five days, but if we travel through the night, we should arrive by tomorrow afternoon."

"Yes, certainly." Sophie put some enthusiasm into her voice, and was rewarded with a smile. She knew Joseph must be worried. Even though the letter had been delivered express, she and Joseph would be arriving at least a week after it was penned.

They were both too tired to care about propriety that night. Sophie lay on the carriage seat with her head resting on Joseph's lap. When she woke during the night, she was relieved to see he'd also fallen asleep, propped against the door, his legs stretched onto the seat opposite and his hands resting in her hair.

The stops during the night and the following day blurred together. Sophie and Joseph never stayed at the inns for more than an hour—only pausing to eat, drink, and refresh their horses. Sophie relished those brief minutes when she could exercise her legs and stretch the muscles in her back. Returning to the carriage became increasingly unpleasant. She didn't complain, and neither did Joseph, but there was no mistaking the note of relief in his voice when he said, "We're nearly there."

Sophie jolted forward, eager for her first glimpse of Kensington. The road was the definition of *untamed*: the forest encroached on both sides, sending roots and vines across the dirt tracks to jolt the carriage and make the horses' progress difficult. Dead and decaying leaves coated the ground, suggesting very few humans passed that way.

They broke through the forest and into long-untended

farmland. Like the road, the fields were partially reclaimed by woods. Sophie caught glimpses of the remnants of crops; little patches of barley poked through the weeds, and an overturned stone trough told her some animal had once pastured in the fields.

Then they began passing dilapidated farmhouses. The empty windows, cold chimneys, and collapsing roofs were far more depressing than Sophie had anticipated.

"So many empty homes…" she murmured. "And no one lives here anymore?"

"Not for a hundred years."

It felt wrong. The people who had built those farmsteads must have been proud of them. Families had been raised there—children born, romances kindled, lives extinguished. But humankind had fled the village, leaving it with nothing but memories and the company of the ever-creeping forest.

They moved past the outskirts and through the center of town. The main street was cobbled, but time had covered the stones with so much dirt that they barely showed.

A few buildings still held signs that swung on groaning chains. The images burned into the rotting wood showed evidence of an apothecary, an inn called the Spotted Horse, and an ironsmith. The other stores had lost their identities to time. Doors and windows hung open, and more than one roof had collapsed. As Sophie peered inside the buildings, she caught sight of abandoned furniture. The disturbing sensation of loss intensified, and she sat back, not wanting to see any more.

Joseph, seeming to sense her discomfort, took out her hand

and pressed it. "Not long now. We have a little more forest to travel before we reach Kensington's border."

His touch lingered, sending prickles over her skin. Sophie, hardly daring to breathe, turned her hand to weave her fingers through his. Joseph didn't meet her smile, but he didn't pull away either.

He's incomprehensible. I almost convince myself I'm no longer dear to him, then he does something like this. What I wouldn't give to understand him just a little.

The trees ahead thinned, and their carriage drew to a halt before Sophie could glimpse any house. Joseph gave her hand a final squeeze then released it. "We'll have to travel the remainder on foot."

Sophie didn't care; anything to get her out of the carriage and bring some life into her legs. She clambered down the steps before Joseph could round the carriage to help her out.

Their driver remained in his seat. His face was pale, but he gave Joseph a curt nod. "One week, sir."

"Thank you." Joseph passed a handful of coins to the driver then stepped back so that the carriage could turn.

Sophie rotated to face the road and felt her breath catch. A patch of trees had been cleared, apparently as an area for coaches to turn about, and beyond that, a black chasm split the earth.

CHAPTER 8
KENSINGTON

"SWEET MERCY," SOPHIE MURMURED.

The gorge was at least thirty paces wide. Vines and straggly shrubs coated the ground leading to its edge, which dropped away sharply. In the failing light, the cliff of somber gray stone looked like a black gash marring the landscape. Sophie took two steps forward but didn't dare get any closer to its edge. She couldn't see the gorge's base.

"A river runs through there," Joseph said. The drop-off didn't seem to faze him, and he regarded it with mild curiosity. "At least, it did eighty years ago. It may have dried by now."

Sophie's attention moved from the chasm to their means of crossing it. A wood-and-rope bridge spanned the dark fall. It looked as though it had once been sturdy enough for a half-dozen carriages to cross at once, but it hadn't been immune to time's patient corruption. The rope was discolored and worn, the upright braces on each side tilted alarmingly, and the wooden slats appeared decayed.

She opened her mouth to object then closed it. *Don't complain. You never asked for or expected this journey to be safe.*

Their carriage had completed its turnaround and halted at the edge of the woods. The driver dismounted to unload their luggage. He moved quickly, as though eager to leave the wilderness and return to civilization, but he stacked the boxes and cases neatly. When the driver finished, he reclaimed his seat and turned to watch them as if he shared Sophie's uneasiness about the bridge.

Joseph approached the drop-off and ran one hand over the rope. Sophie followed closely, terrified that he would slip and fall over the edge, her hands hovering at the ready to grab his coat and pull him back if needed. Joseph's black eyes glittered as he scanned the wood. "It doesn't look pretty, but it bore Garrett's weight at least. I'll cross first; wait here a moment."

Sophie didn't like letting Joseph test the bridge's safety, but she knew it would be irrational to accompany him. While the bridge should be able to survive one person's weight, two might push it past its limits.

Joseph fetched two of their four cases and stepped onto the bridge. Sophie expected him to cross carefully, one step at a time, testing each slat before trusting it to bear him. Instead, he strode across at the same brisk, smooth pace he used when walking through the city. He didn't even look down.

Sophie inhaled a panicked gasp as the rope groaned, but

Joseph reached the opposite side without any dreaded snapping or cracking noises. He placed the cases at his side then turned and nodded for Sophie to follow.

"This is insanity," she whispered, keeping her voice too quiet for the coachman to hear. She took a deep breath and eased one foot onto the first slat.

The wood strained under her boot, and cold sweat broke out over Sophie's skin. She held still for far too long as she gathered her nerves for the second step.

"It's more solid than it looks," Joseph called. She knew he must be impatient though he kept his voice kind. She braced herself for a horrible plunge into the abyss then took the second step.

Again, the wood groaned, and again, it held her weight. Sophie didn't allow herself to stop but used the momentum to carry her forward. The bridge swung as she moved farther from the supports. Its motion combined with fear-induced dizziness to make her feel as though she were about to pitch over the edge. She held her hands toward the rope railing on either side, her fingers hovering an inch over the rough fiber.

As she passed the halfway point, she took her eyes off the wooden slats under her feet and glanced beyond, toward the gorge's floor. The distance was nauseating. She could make out spindly trees, patches of blue flowers and, snaking through the tract's center, a narrow river.

Terror spiked, but she didn't allow her feet to stop. Instead, she fixed her eyes ahead, not even bothering to watch for rotten slats as she locked her gaze on Joseph and used him as a beacon to pull her forward. When she neared the bridge's end, she sped into a run. Joseph caught her and pulled her close.

"Well done," he murmured. "Shh, there's nothing to be frightened of. Would you like to sit a minute?"

"No, I'm fine." Sophie gulped a deep breath. She realized she'd been breathing in shallow gasps, as though drawing in too much air might overload the bridge. She managed a shaky smile at how foolish she must have looked. "Everything's all right now."

Joseph turned and waved to the carriage. The driver waved back then flicked his reins and directed his horses back along their path.

"He'll return for us in a week." Joseph threaded Sophie's arm through his and began leading her into the forest. "But if you need to leave sooner than that, there will be transportation. Garrett will have brought a man and a horse with him at least. Possibly a full carriage."

Sophie didn't trust herself to speak, so she nodded instead. They were following what must have been a path at one point. The only reminders of its existence were the intermittent stones that had been forced out of the ground by roots. The forest rose high around them, blotting out the failing light and alive with animal and bird noises. The boughs looked nothing like the warm green trees she'd passed during the first part of her journey. These giants were dark, gnarled, and ancient. She suspected many of them had been there during Miss Bishop's lifetime.

"At last." Joseph sighed. Red sunset shone through the trees ahead, promising an open area. They pushed through a final scratchy shrub and entered Kensington's grounds.

The house, made from the same gray stone that lined the chasm, rose like a castle ahead of them. The wing on the farthest side had collapsed, but the remainder of the structure appeared sound. Dozens of windows, dull and foggy from generations of neglect, stared over the long-dead garden. Only one of them, the largest window in the north wing's ground floor, held light.

"Garrett is not yet dead, then," Joseph observed dryly, placing emphasis on the *yet*.

Sophie squeezed his arm, as much to comfort him as herself, and matched his pace as they moved toward the vast, tar-black front doors.

The sun had nearly disappeared behind the trees, marring the ground with deep shadows in between streaks of red light, but Sophie tried to take stock of the area as well as she could. It must have once been a busy estate. A gardener's cottage sat near the edge of the forest, and a pile of rotted wood behind the house might have been the stable. Most of the attic rooms would have housed servants—perhaps as many as fifty of them, judging by the size of the estate—and the house was extensive enough to accommodate large parties of guests. The cracked and weed-pocked front steps would have been scrubbed until shining, and the dead sticks spreading out ahead of the house might have been a flower garden. Now the grand building held nothing but death and decay.

They were nearly at the steps when the house's front door was thrown open. Garrett paused in the opening before descending toward them.

While Joseph had the height advantage, his uncle made up for it with girth. A thick gray mustache disguised his mouth's tilt, but Sophie thought he might be smiling. He met Joseph at the lowest step and hugged him fiercely before pulling back to arm's length and scanning his nephew. "Made it in one piece, eh? I'm glad you came. Thank you."

"Of course," Joseph said. "How are things?"

Instead of answering the question, Garrett exhaled and turned to Sophie. She was acutely aware of his dark eyes scanning her, critical, curious, and narrowed in uncertainty. "I see you brought your wife."

"She insisted," Joseph said. Sophie straightened her back and tried to look more capable than she felt.

Garrett's mustache bristled, and for a second, she dreaded his censure. Then he shrugged, smiled, and patted her shoulder so firmly that she reeled. "I wasn't expecting your company, but I'll gladly take whatever help offers itself. I hope you like reading, my dear."

CHAPTER 9
LIGHTS IN HER EYES

GARRETT LED THEM THROUGH Kensington's front doors and waved toward the dilapidated foyer. "I'm afraid I won't be able to offer the hospitality or comfort I would like to, my dear. The house's state is even worse than I was expecting."

"It's quite all right. Please don't worry." Sophie turned her gaze over the moth-eaten rug crumpled against the wall, the discolored and water-stained paintings, and the cobwebs adorning the sconces and banisters. A gigantic, dust-caked chandelier hung from the ceiling, and the windows were so grimy that barely any light reached the floor. "I'm not afraid of dirt."

"How are we situated for food and water?" Joseph set their cases beside the door. "I brought cured meat and crackers for Sophie and me."

Sophie clasped her hands together. She hadn't even thought of food and other supplies; all she'd packed were clothes.

"We'll eat plainly, but we won't starve. I brought food as well, and there is an abundance of wild fowl and edible plants in the forest. And the house has a well that still reaches water." Garrett led them toward the grand staircase at the back of the foyer. While long-dry leaves and dirt coated most of the foyer, the space leading to the stairs was scuffed clean, suggesting that it was traveled frequently. "But whatever we eat we'll have to catch and prepare ourselves. My man never returned from delivering my letter."

Joseph frowned. "Do you have any way to leave—a horse at least?"

"No luck. My man was supposed to ride to the closest town— the closest living town, I should say—pay for the express delivery, and return. But he didn't come back. Until you showed up, I was half-afraid he'd plunged from the bridge and died. But it seems increasingly likely he abandoned us."

Sophie felt a flicker of triumph. With no way to travel to town, Joseph was powerless to send her away. She'd be with him until their carriage returned the following week.

Are we sure that's good news? Sophie ignored the practical voice in the back of her mind as they reached the top of the stairs and followed Garrett down the hallway.

"How's Elise?" Joseph's eyes were constantly moving, darting from shadowed corners to paintings to the half-open doors. Since stepping inside the building, he'd become more alert. The wolf—so familiar to Sophie from her brief stay at Northwood— had awoken.

49

Garrett took a deep, slow breath before replying. "She has good days and days that are…difficult. I was hoping you could talk with her. Seeing you might help."

They'd reached a door at the end of the hall. Garrett knocked then pushed it open without waiting for a reply. Sophie let her husband move in first but followed closely.

The room was cleaner than the rest of the house. Someone had clearly put effort into sweeping out the dust and grime, though it would need a thorough wash and a new layer of wallpaper to be considered respectable. The sheets seemed clean and fresh, at least, and a row of tidy dresses was visible through the wardrobe's open doors.

Elise knelt in the center of the room. Her hair—pitch-black like the rest of her family's—was braided neatly and held in place with a ribbon. Her skin had the same sickly pallor Sophie had noticed in Northwood, but the darkness around her sunken eyes seemed more pronounced. She was thinner and her expression so flat that it was difficult to imagine her smiling. At thirteen, she should have been looking forward to entering society as an adult within a few years. But the Elise that knelt on the wooden floor seemed so wholly soulless—so completely void of joy and energy—that it was hard to imagine her having a future at all. *She's the same age as my brother, and I don't think a single day has passed in the last five years when he didn't laugh at least once. What must she have suffered to make her like this?*

The answer came easily. Scattered about the girl were hundreds of sheets of paper. On each of them was painted the same horribly familiar image: a dark shape shrouded in shadows, clawed fingers raised, mouth open in a snarl. Two points of white existed for its lamp-like eyes.

Garrett crouched in front of his daughter and tapped her chin to get her attention. His voice, which had been gruff before, dropped into a gentle, coaxing tone. "Your cousin has come to visit, my dear. Say hello."

Elise stayed still, and only her sunken eyes moved. They swiveled toward Joseph and locked on him. She maintained the gaze for a moment, neither blinking nor speaking, before her attention turned to Sophie.

As their eyes met, Sophie gasped and took a half step away. Joseph's hand found hers and rubbed it, offering what comfort he could. Sophie clutched back, terrified.

The eyes were Elise's, but buried in their black depths was the familiar cold, vicious light that had haunted her nightmares. *Grimlock.*

Without so much as a twitch, Elise turned back to the page and resumed working the charcoal over it, building a rendition of her captor.

Garrett rose and moved toward them. Bitter grief contorted his face. "I tried taking the charcoal away once," he said, quiet enough that Elise wouldn't hear. "But she bit her finger until it bled and used that instead."

Joseph's fingers twitched in Sophie's hand. Unlike his uncle, Joseph's face remained smooth, but she could feel the anger building in him. "You have a plan." He stated it as fact, not a question.

Garrett sighed. "Of sorts. Let's go downstairs."

Leaving Elise's room felt like coming indoors on a freezing evening. When they crossed the threshold into the hallway, Sophie realized how cold the room had been and how heavily the atmosphere had pressed on her.

Both men seemed absorbed in their thoughts as they followed the hallway back to the stairs and moved to the ground floor. Sophie jogged to match their pace. She was grateful that Joseph hadn't released her hand. Kensington felt so hostile and dead that she needed his touch to remind herself of why she was there.

As they entered the foyer, Garrett turned left, taking them toward the wing where Sophie had seen the light on their arrival. He stopped with one hand on the carved door's handle and looked at Joseph. "You heard, I suppose, that Miss Bishop had plans to conquer the Grimlock before her brother's death."

"Yes. What have you found?"

"I've found many things." Garrett sighed. "Whether they will be any help—well, you'd better see for yourself."

The door groaned on its hinges as he pushed it open, and Sophie's eyes widened as she stepped into the room beyond.

CHAPTER 10
A MAZE MADE OF WORDS

"I SUSPECT MISS BISHOP may have been insane by the time of her death." Garrett stepped aside so Joseph and Sophie could take the room's full measure.

It was a library unlike anything she had seen before. Her father kept a book collection in his study that took up four shelves. One of Sophie's friends had an entire room dedicated to books. And there had been a private library in Northwood that had amazed and delighted her when she'd first seen it.

Miss Bishop's collection easily surpassed all of those other libraries combined. The room was vast and seemed to take up Kensington's entire corner. Windows were set into the two external walls, some overlooking the lawn that led to the crumbling path through the forest, the rest facing the overgrown gardens that ran along the house's sides. Below the windows were reading benches and wooden chairs.

Set into the center of the room and lining every available patch of wall not taken up by windows or doors were floor-to-ceiling bookcases. And every shelf was filled to overflowing with books and papers.

There must be thousands of them. No, more—ten thousand at least.

"The central shelves are mostly books on the occult, magic, cryptozoology, and the like," Garrett said, gesturing. "Those along the back wall are fairy tales. The opposite wall is full of handwritten accounts that, for the most part, seem to be recollections and anecdotes of dealings with the paranormal. It appears that Miss Bishop either traveled to record these testimonies or invited her subjects here so they could share their tales. And at the back are several hundred journals accounting her daily life—her discoveries and defeats."

"I never dreamed so many books on magic existed." Sophie's heartbeat thundered in her ears as excitement and seeping dread fought each other.

Garrett's eyes were cold. "The books are grouped into those rough categories, but if there is any semblance of a filing system, I have not discovered it. Her journals span most of her life, but they aren't stored in order. A book from when she was fifteen might be sitting next to one written when she was sixty. The central shelves—the ones dealing with magic and the occult—contain the most books, but there's no way to tell which might be helpful. Miss Bishop apparently didn't have much regard for bookmarks or tags."

Joseph ran his finger along a row of faded spines as he read the titles. "*Water Nymph Larvae*; *Animal Skins and Their Mythical Application*; *Scientific Theories on the Scottish Boren*…these don't seem very relevant."

"No." Garrett's brows lowered farther, narrowing his eyes into slits. "They don't."

Joseph tilted his head as he studied Garrett's expression. "You believe Miss Bishop purchased any book she could find that related to the supernatural but left no way to track passages that pertain to the Grimlock."

"Yes."

"Which means there may be help for us in these shelves, but it's hidden in a labyrinth of useless volumes."

"You've found the core of my problem, dear nephew." Garrett shifted to lean against one of the reading tables. "My man and I spent five days reading until our eyes blurred, but we didn't find so much as a single helpful snippet. He was becoming sullen and slow, so instead of enduring it, I sent him to fetch you, thinking that an extra pair of eyes would speed our work up by a half. But as we've discovered, my man was honest enough to deliver the letter but clearly had no desire to return here." Garrett nodded toward Sophie. "I'm grateful you've come. Any help you can provide—either here or watching over Elise—is very appreciated."

"Of course." Sophie loved to read. It felt good to know she could be more useful than simply acting as moral support for Joseph. "Whatever you need most."

Joseph ran a hand through his hair as he stepped back to examine the extent of the library. "Where did you start?"

"The journals. I thought that if she had uncovered anything significant, Miss Bishop would have recorded it there. But the last journal we found was from when she was sixty, nearly a decade before her death if my memory serves me." Garrett picked up a small, worn, leather-bound book from the reading desk and shook it so that the yellowed pages fluttered. "In it, she writes of purchasing new books for her collection, of how the town's population is dwindling, and how she is having increasing trouble tracking down a mystic who was supposed to be hiding in the marshes some miles away. She repeatedly mentions her desire to find a weakness in the Grimlock, but her writings contain no breakthroughs."

Joseph took the book and flipped through to its last pages. "And this is the final one?"

"That we could find, yes. She either ceased keeping journals, or the remainder are hidden in the other shelves. They don't contain any markings on their spines, so they would blend in with the other books. I doubt she intended to hide them, but she's done a thorough job regardless."

Garrett was clearly frustrated. He paced the length of the room, arms folded, and scowled at the shelves. "My first four days here were spent searching for and reading the most recent journals. Then my man and I spent the fifth day going through the central shelves to see if we could find a book that dealt with the Grimlock directly. No such luck. In the week that I've been waiting for you, I've been reading the handwritten accounts on the back wall there. They vary wildly in their coherence, and some seem to deal with creatures that are *similar to* but *not quite* the Grimlock. The rest, however, are old wives' tales, fiction, or delusions." He snorted.

"How many have you read?" Joseph asked.

"Nowhere near as many as I would like. The writing is cramped and the ink faded, which makes it slow." Garrett stepped forward and passed his hand over five shelves. "I've read these, and I'm partway through this."

Sophie felt her heart sink. It was a drop in an ocean of words. She looked toward Joseph, afraid to see defeat in his face, but his eyes were keen as they skipped over the shelves. "I suppose you'd better tell us where to start, then."

"Go wherever you think your time is best spent." Garrett moved back to a reading desk that held a stack of loose pieces of paper. "I'll continue with these testimonies, but you're welcome to try the printed books or even the journals. We only read a few of them; it's possible there's something useful in an earlier one." He pointed toward a pot of ink. "When you read a book, leave a mark on its spine. One stripe if you've scanned it quickly, two stripes for reading it thoroughly. Anything that relates to the Grimlock, even if it doesn't appear helpful, can be placed on the desk under that last window."

Sophie turned toward the indicated desk. It was empty.

Joseph gave a brief nod then moved to the central shelf closest to the door. He began scanning the names, running his finger along the spines, and occasionally pulling books out. Sophie followed his cue and started at the opposite end of the shelf.

It was a slow process. The books were old, and many of them had lost their spines, which meant she had to pull them out, open them, and hope they had title pages. If they didn't, she scanned the contents to see if she could ascertain their subject matter.

Some of the books had been professionally printed and were clearly intended to be sold in stores. Others came from small publishing houses that supplied directly to organizations interested in the occult. Still others were handwritten and may have been the only copies ever produced. The late Miss Bishop had been exceptionally thorough in her purchases. That knowledge worried Sophie; if a lifetime of research and this vast library hadn't produced a means to destroy the Grimlock, what hope did they have?

It's different for us. We know the Grimlock in a way that Miss Bishop didn't. She may have overlooked a clue or small mention that gives us the key to purge it from Elise if not kill it.

Every few minutes, she'd find a title that had potential, such as *The Immortals Who Walk Our Earth*, and would take it to a desk. She flipped through the volumes, searched for the word Grimlock or any references to black, lamp-eyed monsters, and then dipped the corner of her handkerchief into the ink and used it to paint stripes across the spines.

She'd processed three of her bookcase's shelves by the time hunger and weariness made it impossible to focus. She stepped back and stretched, rotating her stiff neck and sore arms.

Garrett had finished his stack of papers, marked their bases with two stripes, returned them to the shelf, and brought a fresh pile back to his desk. His brow was furrowed and his eyes glassy, but he continued to read doggedly. Sophie felt a tug of pity. She was exhausted after three hours of reading; what must twelve days have done to him?

She moved among the shelves to look for Joseph. He'd abandoned the printed-book section and was kneeling in front of the journals, his eyes darting over the words as he flipped through each page before discarding the book.

Sophie hesitated to interrupt him. She hadn't eaten since their lunch and was parched, but he seemed completely absorbed in his work. She turned toward the door, wondering if she could find the kitchens on her own and whether Garrett would mind her taking his food, then startled when Joseph stood.

"Is something the matter?" He looked as tired as Sophie felt; shadows circled his eyes, and his hair was messy from having fingers run through it countless times. A flash of understanding lit his face, and he inhaled. "Of course—you haven't eaten yet. Forgive me."

"*We* haven't eaten," Sophie corrected, and Joseph gave her a tired smile.

"True. Garrett?"

The large man leaned back in his chair and raised his arms above his head as he stretched. Sophie could hear the vertebrae in his spine cracking from across the room. "Yes, it's about time for a break. Follow me."

Garrett led them back into the foyer and into the rear section of the house. They passed through the dining room, its long table—big enough to seat a party of forty—still coated with the tattered remnants of a tablecloth. A dozen large crates and travel cases stood against one wall. Garrett nodded at them. "I brought extra sheets and blankets. Make yourselves a bed when you're ready; just tell me which room you choose so I know where to find you in an emergency."

"Oh!" Sophie tugged at Joseph's sleeve. "We forgot our cases by the forest—"

"I brought the ones that contain our clothes," Joseph said with a faint smile, "and I'll collect the rest tomorrow morning."

Sophie's stomach gave an unpleasant lurch as she imagined Joseph crossing the bridge alone. Her mind's eye visualized the ropes—strained once too often—snapping and her husband's black hair whipping about his face as he plunged into the gorge, his lips parted in a gasp of shock—

Joseph, seeing her expression, raised his eyebrows. "It's quite all right. A night's dew won't harm them."

Sophie didn't know whether to laugh or cry. She passed her arm through his and held him close as they entered the kitchen. Faint lines of concern hovered around Joseph's eyes, but he didn't ask for any explanation.

"I really wasn't expecting your company, my dear." Garrett sorted through the jars and cloth-covered shapes on the counter. "I don't have much in the way of proper meals prepared—"

"I'll be happy with anything." That was the truth; she was hungry enough to eat a crust of bread with gratitude.

Garrett set about filling four plates. He'd brought an

assortment of foods with a long shelf life—including crackers, cheese, pickles, and cured meat—but he also had some dark-green plants Sophie didn't recognize. "From the forest," he said, seeing her curious expression. "They're bitter but edible."

Although none of the food was warm, Garrett gave generous portions of it and filled pewter cups with water from a jug by the kitchen's fire. He then took one of the plates and turned toward the door. "I'll take this to Elise. Start without me."

"Thank you." Sophie sat opposite Joseph and peered around the kitchen while she picked at the green leaves. A window set into the back wall had lost its panes, and dirt, leaves, and dead insects littered the ground. Like the rest of the building, the room felt saturated in neglect and loneliness; the pots hung on the wall were rusted into junk, and the oven was cold and empty.

Sophie pictured a plump, middle-aged cook, barking orders to her assistants to ensure Miss Bishop's meal was up to her standards. The image of a busy kitchen like the one in her father's home stood in sharp contrast with the current desolate Kensington. For the first time, she felt the unpleasant lurch of homesickness.

She turned her attention to Joseph to distract herself. His gaze was focused on his plate as he moved the cutlery mechanically, but she could tell his thoughts were elsewhere. He looked horribly gaunt, and the deep sadness, which had disappeared from his expression on their arrival at Kensington, had returned.

"Joseph?" She stretched a hand toward him. "Is everything all right?"

"Of course." He smiled, but the expression didn't touch his eyes. "It's been a long day, that's all."

He didn't take the offered hand. Sophie withdrew it, concern and confusion mingling in her heart as she watched Joseph eat.

Perhaps he is just tired. He hasn't slept much. I should prepare our bed soon to save us the work when we're ready to sleep.

She ate quickly, not tasting much of the food but grateful that there was a lot of it. When Garrett returned, she excused herself to make their bed.

"Sheets are in the cases in the dining room," Garrett said. "Do you need help?"

Sophie had no practice at housekeeping and didn't want to show her inexperience, so she declined. She took one of the spare candles and went in search of the bedding.

She had to hunt through a multitude of cases before she found the sheets Garrett had promised. He seemed to have packed almost enough equipment to furnish a house—which, Sophie supposed, was close to what he needed to do while staying at Kensington. She found folded sheets and blankets in one large trunk and bundled them into her arms together with a packet of matches and spare candles. She then took a lamp, holding it precariously as she tried to keep the sheets from trailing along the floor, and turned to search for the foyer and its staircase.

CHAPTER 11
WARNING

SOPHIE GAVE A SHORT, satisfied nod as she scanned the room. It wasn't glamorous, but thanks to the windows being boarded over, it hadn't suffered from the weather the way many of the other rooms had.

The chamber's furnishings were sparse—just a bed, dresser, wooden chair, and a rug that she easily rolled into the room's corner. Sophie set the blankets on the chair, praying it wouldn't be too dusty, and gave the bed an experimental prod. It was clearly ancient but hadn't decayed as badly as Sophie had feared. There weren't any signs of insect or vermin infestations either. The area surrounding Kensington looked as though it could drop well below freezing during winter, which she thought would help deter pests in the rooms without windows.

Once she was satisfied that the bed wasn't entirely repulsive, Sophie stripped off the shreds that had once been blankets, flipped the mattress, and laid down the clean sheets. She'd never been taught to make a bed—there had never been call for her to—but she'd watched the maids a few times when she was a child, and she tried to replicate the motions she'd seen. The result was a bed that, while not up to any honest family's standards, would at least keep them warm.

Sophie stepped back from her work and let her hands drop. She wished there was something she could do to make the chamber a bit more welcoming. Fresh flowers would work, she thought, or some nice paintings. Even new curtains would have been enough to keep the musty room from looking so grim. *At least we're not expecting to stay long. I suppose the most good I can do is to continue Garrett's work in the library.*

She kicked the old sheets into a bundle in the room's corner and placed the candle and matchstick box on the little table beside the bed. A floorboard groaned, and Sophie turned quickly. The bedchamber was empty. She swallowed, took up the lamp, and left the room, suddenly keen for company.

Shivers crept over her arms as she followed the pathway to the stairs. She'd dressed warmly, but Kensington's temperature plummeted as midnight drew closer. She'd nearly reached the landing when a slamming door made her swivel.

The hallway was quiet, but Sophie became aware of a vivid sensation of no longer being alone. She took a step in the direction of the noise and squinted against the shadows. "Hello?"

A floorboard creaked. Sophie raised her lamp higher, trying to glimpse the presence that seemed to hover just beyond her flame's circle of light. "Joseph? Garrett?"

"*Ha.*" The noise came not from ahead of her but behind.

Sophie swung about, her breath catching in her throat, and saw Elise standing near the end of the hallway. The girl was swaying, her head tilted to one side and her mouth frozen into a smile that held too many teeth and not enough emotion.

Sophie pressed a hand to her thundering heart. "Elise—you startled me—"

She hadn't thought it was possible for the smile to widen, but it did. The lamp-like lights in the back of Elise's eyes flashed as she spoke. "It's such a delight to see you again, my dear."

The voice was Elise's. The words weren't. Sophie licked at dry lips. *Should I call Garrett? Is she dangerous?*

Elise turned, her body moving while her eyes stayed trained on Sophie. "Be wary," she cooed before disappearing into her bedroom and gently closing the door.

The lamp's flame flickered as Sophie's hands shook. Although Elise had gone, she still didn't feel alone. A presence—the same one that had slammed the door—was creeping up behind her. Its skeletal fingers would be stretching toward her neck, pools of shadows clinging to its empty eye sockets, its cracked mouth open to expose rotting, toothless gums. And in a second, the fingers would be fixing about her, their skin so cold and their grip so tight that she would be incapable of drawing breath, incapable of screaming—

Sophie turned, a terrified cry escaping her, to face the empty hallway. She stood unmoving for a moment, light brandished and pulse beating like a war drum, then turned and fled for the stairs.

She made it to the ground floor in a flurry of skirts, her hair shaking free of its careful braid and her lungs starved of oxygen. *Company. I need company.*

Light came through the gap under the library's door. Sophie rushed to it and threw it open. Both Garrett and Joseph started away from their work to stare at her.

They'd built a fire in the grate at the rear of the room. It crackled merrily, cutting through the night's chill and throwing shadows along the shelves. Garrett sat in front of his pile of loose-leaf paper, and Joseph had returned to kneeling by the shelves of journals.

"What's wrong?" Joseph asked, rising in a fluid motion. "You're pale. Did something happen?"

"I'm fine." Sophie put the lamp down and shook her head. "But I, uh—Elise."

Garrett's eyebrows lowered. "What happened? Did she speak?"

"Yes. She—she said it was a delight to see me again—but it wasn't said in a kind way—" She broke off, not sure if Garrett would welcome her opinion, but he only nodded.

"As though the creature were speaking through her."

"Exactly." Sophie exhaled. "And she—*it*—said I should be wary."

"Is she still wandering?"

"I don't think so. She went into her room."

Garrett let a lungful of air out in a huff. "I'm afraid she's been saying and doing a lot of strange things. Sometimes it seems like my daughter is present and aware. At other times, it's as though she's nothing but a puppet for that monster."

His voice devolved into a growl for the final sentence. Sophie dropped her eyes. She didn't know what to say; comfort would be repulsive, and commiseration could only hurt him. So instead, she did the only thing that might help and turned to the shelves she'd been working through.

Joseph watched her for several minutes, but Sophie pretended not to feel his eyes on her, and he didn't speak.

They continued their search for hours, pausing only to add fresh wood to the fire and cut their candles' wicks. Around two in the morning, a quiet tapping disturbed Sophie. She raised her attention from the book she'd been pursuing and saw specks of rain glistening on the window. The specks turned into rivulets as the sky unloaded its burden. She shivered and returned to the book.

Her fingertips were stained black from ink, and a headache throbbed at the back of her skull. When she'd finished the tome without yield and returned it to the shelf, she paused to take stock of their progress. It was crushingly small.

We don't need to read every book in this room, she reminded herself. *We just have to find the one that will help.*

The cruel voice in the back of her mind breathed life into the possibility that it was a pointless, fruitless search—that there *was* no help—but she crushed the idea. It was their best hope, so she clung to it with every scrap of determination she had.

She brought a new book back to the reading desk, took her seat, propped her left elbow on the table, and rested her forehead on her palm. She opened the book.

What is its name, again? Arthurian Myths and Legends? *Do I really expect to find help hidden in here?*

The words blurred on the page. Her eyelids fell. Then she jerked away from the desk as her head fell off the propped arm.

She blinked furiously. Her eyesight was still blurred, and every fiber of her body begged for sleep, but she didn't want to leave the room while the men still worked.

A hand pressed onto her shoulder. Sophie looked up to see that Joseph had approached her silently. "It's late. Come. The books will still be here in the morning."

Sophie rose obediently and let Joseph place her hand on his arm. She looked behind them to where Garrett still bent over a stack of paper, deep furrows built around his eyes as he read. He flicked his hand toward them. "Go on. I'll stay here a little longer."

"Good night," Sophie said then followed Joseph out of the room and toward the staircase.

Their candle's flame threw deep shadows over Kensington's walls and ceiling. The falling rain created a steady thrum on the shingles above them, and somewhere deep in the building, a door creaked. Echoing drips testified to the presence of scores of holes in the roof.

Sophie tightened her hand over Joseph's arm. She normally loved rain and found its sounds soothing, but that night, the muted drone set her nerves on edge. *Bleak.* The word seemed to describe the house perfectly. *Everything about this place is bleak.*

Joseph paused on the threshold of their room. "Can I bring you anything tonight? Your luggage or some water perhaps?"

"Thank you, but I'll take care of all of that in the morning." She gave him a tight smile. "I feel like I'll drop dead if I don't sleep soon."

He chuckled as he turned back to the hallway. "Then I'll bid you good night."

"You're leaving?" Sophie caught his sleeve as a pang of fear ran through her. "But—"

He turned his eyes on her, and she fell into the deep pools of sadness lingering there. He was unhappy about something; she just couldn't guess what. "I would like to keep searching a while longer. But if you like, I could stay until you fall asleep."

Don't be weak. She forced herself to release her grip on his arm. *You're not a coward. Don't waste his time by asking to be coddled.* "No, that's not necessary. I only thought—you look so tired—"

He cupped her cheek in his palm, his thumb running over the plume of color she felt spreading out from his touch. "I couldn't sleep right now. But thank you."

"Oh, I see." Sophie was painfully aware of the drum of rain, mournful and deep, against the window. Wind howled through the gaps in the roof and broken windowpanes. For a crazy second, she considered accompanying him back to the library, just to avoid being alone, but had to reject the idea. She was too tired to read coherently. Her presence would only be an inconvenience. "Good night," she said and then on impulse added, "dear Joseph."

His lips twitched into a ghost of a smile. His thumb circled her cheek a final time, then he let go, stepped back, and closed the door.

69

Sophie stood there for a moment, shivering against the freezing air, her only source of comfort the candle she clutched. A deep, cracking sound that echoed from outside the boarded window told Sophie one of the forest's trees had been bowed by the storm's energy. She swallowed and placed her candle on the table pressed close to the bed. There wasn't much wick left—enough to last twenty minutes perhaps—and Sophie decided to let it burn so that she wouldn't have to fall asleep in the dark.

She kicked her boots off and then crawled into the bed fully clothed. She was so bone-weary that even pulling the blankets up to her chin was a chore, but persistent fear refused to let sleep draw close enough to consume her. She rolled over and shivered. The bed was still cold, and unheated by a fire, the air bit at her cheeks. She squeezed her eyes tightly closed and tried to ignore the rain's melancholy drone.

Her room's door creaked as it opened. Sophie turned over, hoping Joseph might have changed his mind and come to bed, but her visitor hadn't brought any light, and Sophie's own candle was too weak to penetrate the darkness lingering about the door.

"Hello?" Sophie sat up, pulling her sheets up to her chin, and squinted into the shadows. A figure moved there—too short to be Joseph, too tall for Elise, and too thin for Garrett.

Her tiredness vanished. Sophie reached for the candle on her bedside table, but her hands shook badly, and she bumped the candlestick. It fell to the floor, spilling wax and dousing the flame.

Sophie's breath froze in her lungs. She held still, listening. There was the beat of rain, heavier than before, as the storm grew.

Her heartbeat throbbed in her ears. And half-disguised under the other noises was the sluggish, rattling breath of her visitor.

She threw her torso over the side of the bed, both hands searching the floor. A finger touched the candleholder's metal, and she grabbed the precious light then pulled back and sat up in the bed. She didn't dare take her eyes off the patch of darkness where she'd last seen the visitor. One hand searched to her right, fingers creeping over the wooden desk until they found the matchbox she'd placed there earlier that evening.

She couldn't stop shaking. Matches spilled over the bedcovers when she opened the box, but that didn't matter. She only needed one. She struck it and could have cried when it didn't flare. Another strike, and then a third, and at last the precious, precious light bloomed, giving her a narrow circle of illumination. She touched the match to the wick. The wax was still warm, and the candle hissed into life. She raised it, leaning as far forward as she dared, so that the flickering light drew the intruder out of its heavy casing of shadows.

She screamed.

CHAPTER 12
THE VEILED LADY

THE FIGURE STOOD AT the foot of her bed, so close that she could have touched it if she'd just shifted forward a little. It was a woman, taller than Sophie and far gaunter. Her dress was a deep-black satin—rich and detailed enough to testify to the owner's wealth and clearly intended for mourning. Her fingers, long and skeletal, gripped the bed's end. A long black veil hung from her elaborately dressed black hair but had been pulled back to expose her face.

The woman was dead. Her aged and withered skin clung to the fiercely pronounced cheekbones and chin. The cracked lips hung open, allowing empty breaths to rattle through her mouth. Sophie instinctively knew the woman's gaze was fixed on her, but the eyes were sightless; nothing remained but empty, shadowed sockets.

The scream died as her lungs ran out of oxygen. Sophie tried to pull back, to crawl away from the morbid figure, but that abrupt jerk was her undoing. The candle's flame was still too fresh to survive the motion. Darkness swept through the room as the light died.

No! Sophie scrabbled for another match from those she'd spilled over the bed, but the small wooden sticks slipped through her fingers as she fought to control her shaking hands.

A beating noise was growing closer, almost matching her pulse in tempo. *Footsteps*, Sophie realized. Her fingers seized a new match and fumbled to strike it.

The flame caught at the same moment as the door was thrown open. Sophie stared at the foot of her bed where the veiled woman had stood no more than five seconds before. She hadn't heard the figure move, but it had disappeared, seemingly dissolving into the night.

Someone was shaking Sophie's shoulders. She blinked and looked toward the person crouched at the side of her bed. Joseph's eyes, pitch-black and wild, met hers. "What happened?" he barked. "Are you hurt?"

"Th-th-th-th—" Sophie tried to explain, but the words stuck in her throat. She couldn't look away from her husband's face. "A-a-a—*woman*—"

Joseph's gaze flicked toward the match, and he hissed. One of his hands came to hers and snuffed out the flame, which had burned low enough to blister Sophie's fingers.

How strange; I didn't even feel it.

The room swam around Sophie. She keeled forward, trying to reach toward Joseph but unable to move her hands. He caught her.

Consciousness bled in and out. She was aware of movement and gentle, cushioned bumps as they descended the stairs. There were voices too, one sharp and familiar, the other deep and solemn. Then the motion ceased, the voices quietened, and something cold and wet was pressed to Sophie's forehead.

She forced her eyes open. Joseph was kneeling beside her as he dabbed a wet cloth over her face.

"There was a woman." Her tongue felt sluggish and heavy. "A dead woman."

"Shh." He took the cloth away and replaced it with his fingers as he felt her skin. His face darkened. "You're feverish. I shouldn't have let you work so hard or so long."

"No. I'm perfectly fine." Sophie struggled to sit up, but Joseph pushed her back down. She was in a parlor, she realized, and had been laid on an ancient chaise longue. A thick coat had been draped under her to keep her from resting directly on the decaying furniture. "There was someone in my room."

Joseph frowned. "Elise?"

"An old woman." Sophie squeezed her eyes closed at the memory. "She was dead. No eyes. Dressed all in black—she was standing at the foot of the bed—"

She knew she sounded crazy, but Joseph didn't try to argue. He pressed his hand to his mouth, his frown deepening. "Garrett, have you seen a woman in this house?"

"No." Sophie turned toward the voice and saw Garrett lighting a fire in the room's grate. He looked grave. "But it sounds like the Grimlock's influence."

"It could raise the dead at Northwood," Joseph said, more to himself than to his companions. "But I thought that was because the bodies were given to it as a sacrifice."

"We'd know for certain if we could only find some help in that damn library." Garrett's voice grew louder with each word. He kicked at the stone fireplace, knocking a layer of soot free. "If that damn woman had *labeled her books*—"

Sophie shrank back, her anxiety growing as Garrett's face contorted in barely contained fury.

"Be civil," Joseph snapped then softened his voice as he stroked the loose hair away from Sophie's face. "Don't be afraid, my dear."

Garrett rubbed his hands through his hair, making the gray-streaked locks poke up at odd angles, then he sighed so heavily that he seemed to deflate. "Apologies."

He's frustrated and desperate. I would be too if Elise were my daughter. Sophie's gaze moved to the fire, which was growing brighter as it caught on the logs. The sensation of eyes watching her made her look toward the dark space above the mantel. She gasped and started upright, clutching at Joseph's arm. "It's her—it's the woman!"

Joseph and Garrett turned in the direction Sophie stared, toward the large painting over the fireplace. An elderly woman contemplated the room through proud steel-gray eyes. Her hair, drawn into a harsh bun, matched her ink-black mourning dress. The painting was of a living woman, but her facial shape—high cheekbones and sharp chin—was too distinct for there to be any doubt. The woman depicted in the painting had visited Sophie's room.

Joseph exhaled. "Miss Bishop. I should have guessed."

CHAPTER 13
WATER

SOPHIE SLIPPED HER LEGS over the edge of the chaise longue, senseless to Joseph's objections as she stared at the image. She could tell Miss Bishop would have been a severe, hardened woman in life. She seemed close to sixty in the painting, which was near the end of her life. She looked far from frail, though. The artist had caught the sharp, arrogant glint in the woman's eyes, and the creases around her brow and lips hardened her appearance.

Sophie licked her lips as she tried to reconcile the stately figure above the mantel with the lifeless, bloodless phantom in her room. *How did Miss Bishop come back?* At Northwood, Marie, her murdered maid, had been able to pass on once the Grimlock's grip on the building was broken. Miss Bishop must have scorned the afterlife, and her spirit had lain dormant in Kensington for more than a hundred years until the Grimlock gave it form.

"Sophie." The voice, soft but worried, permeated her thoughts. Sophie startled as Joseph ran his hand over her shoulder. "Are you well?"

"Yes, fine, thank you." The anxious lines around Joseph's eyes didn't abate, though, and she tried to smile to reassure him.

"Would you like to move to a different room? There's no place to lie down in the library, but I'm sure we can—"

"No." The decisiveness in Sophie's voice surprised even her, but she knew it was the right choice. "I'm not afraid of her. I'll stay here."

It's only a painting, not the real thing. There's no room for senseless fear in Kensington.

Joseph scanned her face, seeming to test her sincerity, then he nodded. "As long as you're comfortable. I'll keep you company tonight."

Garrett appeared in the doorway, an assortment of blankets, pots, and cups balanced in his arms. Sophie hadn't been aware of his leaving. He handed the blankets to Joseph then poured them three cups of tea. "We have no milk, I'm afraid, but this will keep us warm if nothing else."

Sophie took hers gratefully. Joseph draped two of the blankets about her shoulders then sat next to her while Garrett flopped into the chair opposite.

None of them spoke, and they stayed wrapped in their thoughts as tiredness crept back over Sophie. She didn't realize she was falling asleep until Joseph took the half-empty cup from her hands and eased her back onto the chaise longue.

"I'm fine," she mumbled as Joseph tucked the blankets around her.

"Shh, close your eyes. I'll watch over you."

Her dreams were innocent enough to begin with. She was walking through a forest, delighted by the sunlight-speckled boughs and profusion of flowers. Footsteps followed her, but she couldn't remember who her companion was. As she stopped to touch a tree trunk, a rattling, scraping breath made her gasp. She turned to face her follower, but the path was empty. Again the breath came, this time echoing all about her. Sophie rotated, preparing to run for home, but found her way blocked by the tall, glowering woman. She tried to speak, to retreat, to raise her hands to protect herself, but her movements were sluggish and weak. She was no longer in the green forest but back in Northwood, the red-and-gold walls looming close and threatening to smother her—

She startled awake. It was morning; thin, joyless sunlight stretched through the windows. Garrett had left, but Joseph remained, sitting on the ground near her head, his long legs stretched across the wooden floor. He turned when she stirred. "Ah, you're awake. Good. How do you feel?"

Sophie opened her mouth to answer then caught sight of his face. She reached toward him, her hand stopping just short of touching his skin, as anxiety twisted her insides. "You look exhausted. Did you get any rest last night?"

"A few hours while Garrett kept watch." Joseph leaned away from her hand then stretched and rose. "He made us a breakfast of sorts. Would you like me to heat some water so you can wash?"

Sophie stood as well and pulled the blanket around herself. She couldn't stop examining Joseph's pale appearance but managed to smile. "Thank you. Cold water will be fine—I'll take care of it." She glanced toward the door then gave him an apologetic grin. "If you would be kind enough to tell me where to find the water…?"

"Hm." He motioned toward the doorway. "The well is in the basement. Follow me."

He led her from the parlor and toward the back of the house. The hallways became narrower and the furnishings plainer as they left the public section of the mansion and entered the servants' realm. Sophie could feel Joseph's gaze on her as they walked, but she couldn't guess the cause of his attention until he spoke.

"Last night's events concerned me." He seemed to be phrasing his words carefully. "Garrett and I discussed it after you fell asleep. We agreed that it is likely Miss Bishop is not under the Grimlock's control. She was not included in the Argenton pact, and her body was not tied to him on death, so he should have no influence over her reanimated form. However, that does not mean she is friendly." He paused and shot her a sharp look. "I would like you to be careful."

She blinked at him. "Of course I will. I hope you don't think I'm the reckless type. I get my thrills through books."

"Ha!" His laugh was short, but he seemed genuinely amused. "That's what I assumed until you argued and bargained and threatened so passionately to join this mad expedition."

"Oh. Well—I suppose—" Sophie could feel herself turning pink. "That is—"

They'd entered a cellar and had to change to single file to climb down the stone stairs. Joseph waited until they'd reached the floor before resuming the conversation. "That wasn't a criticism. Only a caution." The amusement died from his face. "As dearly as I wish I could whisk you away from here, the three of us are trapped for the week. So I would like you to promise me, my dear, that you will place your own safety above everything else. Even above *my* well-being."

Sophie opened her mouth but couldn't speak. Joseph's eyes, so dark that they could have been cut out of a starless night sky, transfixed her.

"I know why you accompanied me." His voice was a whisper, but it echoed strangely through the basement. "You came for my sake. But that can no longer be your priority."

"You…" She felt as if she were drowning in the intensity of his stare. His hand came to caress the tender skin under her chin, and she shuddered.

"It was foolish of me to let you come, and it would destroy me if my carelessness resulted in your injury or—" His voice cracked. He took a deep breath to regain control. "Or your death. You *must* leave Kensington. Even if you leave alone."

Sophie didn't dare take her eyes off his but felt for his hand blindly. She found it and grasped it with all of the strength she could muster. "Don't talk like that. We'll both walk out of here. And Garrett and Elise too."

"I wish I had the luxury of your optimism, my darling."

She brought his hand to her lips and kissed the knuckles.

The touch brought a sigh from him, but instead of closing the distance between them, he pulled back. Tears pricked at Sophie's eyes as Joseph slipped his fingers out of hers.

"What is it?" Her voice was breaking, but she'd gone too far to stop. "I know something's wrong. You look sad all of the time, and you're so pale. And I—I don't know—if you feel anything for me—"

"Promise me you will be safe. I can endure all else if I am only assured of that."

He was asking for the impossible. She couldn't guarantee her own well-being any more than she could vouch for his. But she gave him as much as she was capable of: "I will be careful." *In the same way that I care for you.*

He nodded and closed his eyes. When he opened them again, his face was clear and his voice brisker. "It would be wise if you stayed close to either Garrett or me, especially at night."

"Of course." Sophie licked her lips. She'd given Joseph what he wanted—her promise of caution—but without receiving a response to her own request. She hadn't imagined it would be possible to feel so conflicted. His worry for her, his urgent appeal that he kept her company during the night—they told her that she was dear to him. But his distance, his reluctance to hold or kiss her, and his careful avoidance of the subject cast strong doubt.

He's a principled man. Is it possible he feels responsible for me in the same way he cares for Elise? Does he see it as his duty to protect me even if he doesn't love me?

The thought moved from her mind to her stomach, where it twisted into a cold knot. She suddenly felt sick and clutched the blanket around her tightly before following Joseph to the well at the back of the basement.

CHAPTER 14
OLD SECRETS

THEY BROUGHT THE WATER upstairs in large pitchers. Once he'd confirmed she didn't need anything else, Joseph left to retrieve the remainder of their luggage from the other side of the chasm. Sophie tried not to think of him crossing the bridge while weighed down by cases but instead focused on washing as quickly as she could. The water felt like barely thawed ice, and she was shaking by the time she started dressing.

Joseph returned while she was tying her hair back and accompanied her to the library. Garrett was already immersed in his stack of papers. He waved vaguely and grunted as they entered, and Sophie saw he was indicating two plates that sat on a table. He'd prepared helpings of cured meat and buttered bread.

Joseph took his plate and knelt in front of the wall full of diaries. He was soon immersed in the cramped writings, occasionally raising a slice of bread to his mouth. Sophie stayed by the table as she ate and let her eyes rove over the walls of books.

Garrett's frustrated cry from the day before came back to her. "If that damn woman had *labeled her books*—"

The proud, severe woman in the painting didn't seem like the sort to suffer foolishness or whimsy. She wasn't the eccentric, vague scholar Sophie had imagined when she'd first seen the library but someone who'd behave with pin-neat precision. It did seem very odd that her books were arranged so haphazardly.

Sophie glanced toward the table where they were supposed to collect any books that referenced to the Grimlock. It was bare. *Not a single find after nearly a fortnight of searching.*

Revelation crashed over her, making her inhale sharply. She blinked and placed her half-eaten breakfast to one side. *No, don't become too excited. It's not a certainty, only a theory.*

But if her theory was right...

She turned to Joseph to tell him she needed to go upstairs, but the phrase died on her tongue. He was focused on a passage, his lips twitching as he silently mouthed the words. *It's not worth disturbing him for what might be a fool's errand.*

She turned toward Garrett. His hands were dug into his dark hair as he scowled at the papers. Like Joseph, his pose and expression didn't invite interruption.

Sophie went to the door, opened it, and slipped outside without attracting either man's attention. She paused in the foyer and surveyed the vast, decayed room.

Where should I start? Not a public room—she wouldn't keep it anywhere a curious guest might disturb. Perhaps in her bedroom or a private study.

She moved up the stairs and glanced along the hallway. She hadn't seen the master bedroom the night before when she'd been searching for a room to sleep in, but most likely, it overlooked the front yard.

The hallway to her left stretched away for twenty feet before splitting. Sophie knew that farther along, past a few more turns, the passageway would cease to exist. That side of Kensington had collapsed into a pile of bricks and crushed furniture. She hoped Miss Bishop's room wasn't in the demolished section.

The hallway to her right was shorter. The room at the end was Elise's, so Sophie eschewed it and began opening other doors. The first few chambers were empty or had minimal furniture covered in white sheets, but the fourth door let her into the master bedroom.

The room was large and decorated in subdued, faded browns and greens. The bed's curtains had collapsed, and the carpet was eaten away. Despite those obvious signs of age, Sophie knew the room had once been immaculate. The furniture was minimal but high quality and without flourishes. The only adornment was a painting hung above the fireplace. It depicted a young, golden-haired man. He was smiling as he posed in outdated clothes, and Sophie tilted her head as she examined it. *Is that her brother, Thomas Bishop?*

There wasn't much to see in the room besides chairs arranged about the fireplace, a wardrobe, a writing desk, and the bed. A second door was set beside the fireplace, though, and Sophie—hoping for a study or a storage room—opened it. She was disappointed to find herself in a dressing room. The clothes were moth-eaten and decayed but still mostly intact. She searched through the area without finding anything noteworthy.

Then a thought struck her, and she turned back to the main room. *Why have a wardrobe in your bedchamber when you also have a dressing room?* She crossed to the tall wooden cupboard and wrenched the doors opened.

"Yes!"

She didn't try to stifle the delighted cry. The wardrobe didn't store clothes but held shelves. And on them were a dozen neat, carefully arranged books and a stack of loose-leaf papers.

Sophie couldn't believe she hadn't guessed the truth earlier. The downstairs library didn't, and never had, stored any information on the Grimlock. It was simply a place for Miss Bishop to put the books she had no use for—a literary graveyard. She'd kept her important collection—the relevant books—close at hand.

No wonder Garrett found nothing despite a week of searching.

Sophie let her hand drift over the spines as she read their names. The top shelf held diaries. Without even opening them, she knew they would be from the final decade of Miss Bishop's life—the years missing from downstairs. Below those were eight books, most of them hand bound. One felt familiar, though, and Sophie pulled it free. *Cryptids and the Occult*—the book her father had bought when she was a child.

Below that shelf was a small stack of handwritten accounts.

Sophie guessed that, unlike the library's piles, these would be helpful.

She carried her book, *Cryptids and the Occult*, to the window. Thick clouds dampened the natural light, and rain, no longer the tumultuous storm of the night before but a light shower, continued to paint streaks on the windowpane. Sophie held the book close to the glass so that the light, as much as there was of it, would hit the pages.

Long-dead memories resurfaced as she flipped through the tome. She'd been young when her father had handed her the book among volumes of fairy tales, and the gruesome illustrations had fueled her nightmares for weeks. *There's the entry on the creation of a vengeful ghost.* The image depicted a wealthy woman standing over the corpse of her sister, ax clasped in both hands, as she stared at the severed head rolling about her feet.

The picture was too small and too ill defined to impart any identity to the features, but the woman's pose conjured memories of Joseph's cruel aunt, Rose. Sophie moved on quickly.

There were passages on shadow-walkers, bogrots and resurrectionists. And there, near the end of the book, was the section Sophie had been desperate to reread. *Grimlock*, the title read and below that, *Strike a Deal with the Devil.*

The Grimlock's brief entry took up the left side of the page, and an illustration filled the right. The picture was almost entirely black but showed a looming silhouette with two white, lamp-like eyes.

Sophie's skin crawled, and she snapped the book closed. She

suddenly regretted not asking Joseph to accompany her upstairs. The rain was thickening, creating a sheen of distortion between Sophie and the forest. She bent forward to see the dead garden. Plants were sloughing free from the ground as soil washed down the pebble pathway. Evidently, Kensington wasn't used to this kind of prolonged rainfall.

Movement drew Sophie's attention to a patch of dirt near the forest's edge. A figure stood hunched against the rain and stared at the ground. Sophie frowned and pressed her forehead to the cold glass as she strained to see the figure. *Joseph? Surely he wouldn't have gone outside—*

Lightning flashed, coating the scene in harsh light in the same moment the figure turned and raised its head toward Sophie.

Miss Bishop.

Sophie gasped and jerked away from the window. The light faded only to be followed by a deep crash of thunder. The windowpane rattled, and its noise shook Sophie out of her stunned trance. She turned to the door, took a deep breath, and called, as loudly as she could, "Joseph! Garrett!"

When she turned back to the window, the phantom had vanished. It was almost possible to think the rain had melted it and washed it into the puddles gathering around the trees' roots.

Footsteps echoed in the hallway. Sophie crossed to the door and wrenched it open just as Joseph reached it. He gripped her shoulders, his face hardened in worry as he looked her over. "Are you hurt?" he asked, the harsh bark back in his voice.

"No, no, I'm fine. I didn't mean to alarm you. I'm sorry."

Warm golden light bloomed through the room as Garrett followed Joseph, his lamp held aloft. He gripped a hunting rifle in his spare hand and cast a critical eye over the sparse furnishings.

"What happened?" Joseph smoothed a stray curl away from Sophie's neck. She didn't know if it was her imagination, but she thought his fingers trembled. She pressed a hand to his chest and brushed it to soothe him.

"I saw the woman through the window. It shocked me—I didn't mean to sound so urgent when I called you."

Joseph sighed, and the tension fell out of his posture. "You shouldn't have left without saying something."

"I had a suspicion I wanted to check." A cautiously excited smile tugged at her lips. She offered the book to Joseph. "Look; it's Miss Bishop's private library."

"Sweet mercy," Garrett breathed. He was staring at the cabinet of books. He dropped his lamp onto the desk and began pulling volumes out, handling them with far less care than their age recommended. "Could it really be—"

"Of course. She separated the books that mentioned the Grimlock." The hungry light was back in Joseph's eyes. He took *Cryptids and the Occult* then caught Sophie's hand before she could withdraw it. "Clever, Sophie. Very clever."

Heat rushed through her at the words. She beamed.

"Though I wish you'd told me *before* exploring the house alone," Joseph added, a note of warning slipping into his voice. Then he pressed her hand and matched her smile. "That aside— well done. You've saved us a lot of heartache."

Garrett already had the books out and spread over the desk as he thumbed through two at a time, eagerly searching the entries. "Ah!" he cried, jabbing a page with his finger. "*The Grimlock, also known as Blackthorn and Shadow Deceiver, is a mythical figure renowned for making bargains with mortals, most commonly for their souls. As with most accords struck with immortals, the agreements are traditionally one-sided and result in suffering, death, or the loss of something precious.* That's all it says. Still, it's better than what we had."

Joseph went to the cupboard and brought out a bundle of journals. "*These* are arranged chronologically, thank mercy. I'll check through her most recent entries; tell me if you find anything significant in the books."

The following hour was spent working through the miniature library. When they found a passage on the Grimlock, Garrett or Sophie read it aloud then placed the book, open at the relevant page, on the floor. Most of the books contained no more information than Garrett's first discovery: they identified the Grimlock's role as a being that struck tragic deals with desperate souls, and sometimes they recounted stories, mostly set in medieval times. In the end, the most helpful book turned out to be *Cryptids and the Occult.* Sophie read the short passage aloud for a second time.

"*The Grimlock, a haunt of dead woods, persuades the unwary traveler to strike a wondrous deal. It promises health and wealth, but the price cannot be accounted for. Once the deal has been accepted, the unfortunate body must endure the consequences for longer than the duration of his life. Spears and arrows will not harm the Grimlock. Destroy its heart—that which ties it to the mortal realm—in order to bring about its death.*" She took a deep breath. "When I was a child, I thought the heart was literal. But it seems to be whatever vessel the monster lives in."

She didn't dare meet Garrett's eyes but could feel them boring into her, silently challenging her, as she laid the book back on the table. The implications were clear. *Elise is its heart now. In order to kill the Grimlock, we would have to kill Elise.*

Sophie thought of the sallow, quiet girl who looked so near death already, and she shivered. The idea of murdering her was abhorrent—reprehensible enough that Sophie doubted she could ever forgive herself if she allowed it to happen—yet it was the only apparent solution.

Joseph didn't speak, but his brows were lowered and lips drawn into a tight line. A diary lay open in his hands, but he wasn't reading it.

"No one wants to voice what we're all thinking, eh?" Garrett burst out of his seat. "I swear, I would kill the both of you before I let you draw so much as a drop of blood from my daughter."

"Calm down." Joseph's voice was gentle, but there was a commanding edge to it.

Garrett rounded on his nephew as lightning flashed through the window. "You were thinking about it. Don't try to deny it; I know you were."

"Of course I was." Joseph's volume rose to match his uncle's. "The book told us, in as many words, that we can kill the Grimlock by killing Elise. Yes, I was thinking about it, but you're a fool if you assume I was considering it."

Garrett slumped back against the wall, and his dark eyes turned toward Sophie.

She shrank away from the accusatory glare. "I don't want to see her harmed either."

Joseph placed his journal on the table and leaned forward in the chair. "No one here does. We're going to find an alternative. We must either discover a way to expel the Grimlock, kill it without harming Elise, or coax it into a new vessel." He tapped the book. "Perhaps you would like to hear the theory Miss Bishop was working on before her death."

"Yes," Sophie said, grateful for the change in subject. She drew the spare chair up beside Joseph. Garrett came up on his other side as Joseph opened the journal.

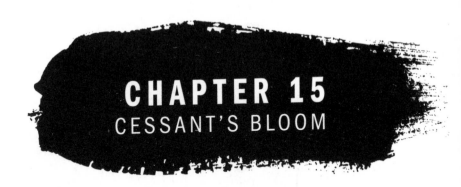

CHAPTER 15
CESSANT'S BLOOM

JOSEPH SHIFTED SO THAT both of his companions could read the journal's cramped notes. "Let me give some context first. As far as I can tell, this is the diary Miss Bishop used during the year preceding her death. By that point, the town was deserted and Miss Bishop had dismissed almost all of her staff. She stayed at Kensington with one lone assistant, Mr. Trent. I believe he was once a footman but worked as Miss Bishop's second-in-command."

Sophie tried not to look shocked. "She kept a male assistant, not a woman?"

"Yes—and I suspect she had a very particular motive for doing so." Joseph flipped back to midway through the book and began reading. "*Mr. Trent stayed awake through the night to assist me in the translation of an ancient text that was loaned us. The pages proved fruitless, but if he was disheartened, he did not show* it. *Truly, I have been fortunate in my companion.*" He turned the pages. "*Mr. Trent returned this morning. He was away for eight days total; the journey has taxed him greatly, but he gives me nothing but smiles. I confess I worry for him when he journeys to retrieve these books—but there is no one else I can trust.*" Another handful of pages turned. "*I dismissed the last two maids today. Now only Mr. Trent and I remain. I do not feel as lonely as I'd feared. John is a great comfort.*"

"Oh." Sophie exhaled. She understood all too well. "She loved Trent."

"She never says as much, but the implications are clear. And it seems that Mr. Trent loved her in return."

"And?" Garrett's gruff voice broke through Sophie's reverie. "You said she had a plan?"

"A lead." Joseph turned to the final pages of the book. "It may prove fruitless, but—"

Garret tilted his head forward and raised his eyebrows in a wordless demand.

"Partway through the journal, Miss Bishop begins talking about a plant, cessant's bloom. I've yet to find any reference to what it does, but during her final year of life, she directed almost all of her focus on searching for it."

"Oh! Wait a moment!" Sophie bolted out of the chair so quickly that it nearly turned over. Mumbling apologies, she crossed to the table and picked up one of the books: *Exceptional Botany*. It was the only volume in Miss Bishop's library that didn't seem to contain any mention of the Grimlock. Sophie had assumed she'd glossed over a brief reference and had set it aside to comb through more thoroughly later.

She opened it carefully, wary of the book's incredible fragility as the spine groaned and the pages crackled, and began hunting through it. She found the passage she was seeking near the end of the book, "*Cessant's Bloom: Herbalist's Miracle.*"

"Here," she said, holding it out for her companions to read with her. "*This blue-flowering plant is as prized as it is rare. Widely regarded as myth but with enough anecdotal records to suggest this mundane-skinned miracle truly exists, cessant's bloom is renowned for healing a vast range of afflictions. The botanist credited with its discovery, Hans Bastion, described it as an herb 'to make what is broken whole.'*"

Sophie raised her head from the book. Joseph met her eyes, and she saw her own excitement reflected back at her.

"Able to make what is broken whole," he echoed. "Is it possible it might separate the Grimlock from Elise?"

Garrett didn't seem to be breathing. One of his hands gripped the back of Joseph's chair so tightly that the wood creaked. "Tell me Miss Bishop writes of where to find it. I beg of you."

Joseph turned to the very last page in Miss Bishop's journal. The neat black ink script stopped partway down the leaf, and nestled between it and the book's back cover was a carefully folded letter. Joseph took it out of its sheath and opened it. The paper was so fragile that little flakes broke off despite his care.

"*Miss Bishop,*" he read. "*Once again, I must insistently refuse your request for a meeting. In addition, I beg that you instruct your lackey to cease his pursuit. I am a retiring man, and I have no wish to be dragged into whatever chaos you're tangled in.*

"You wish to have possession of cessant's bloom seeds. You are correct; I do own some—though how you guessed they had been gifted to me is a mystery. I have never spoken of them and have kept them well hidden.

"I will not meet with you, your assistant, or anyone associated with you. However, in the interests of relieving myself of your attentions, I have left a pouch containing the three seeds hidden in the secret nest under the odd cow's crooked step. You are familiar with the town; I have no doubt you will understand my meaning.

"I pray this will bring about a cessation of your highly irregular and aggressive solicitations.

"Somewhat sincerely, E.D."

"And what does Miss Bishop say?" Sophie asked, trying to read the journal's final entry. "Did she retrieve the seeds?"

"The date of her final entry matches that of the letter," Joseph said, "though she makes no mention of the note or the seeds."

Garret exhaled and rubbed his hands over his face, his frustration clear.

"What could it mean?" Sophie sat back in her chair and rotated her neck, which was developing a crick from the afternoon of reading. "The letter must have come after she wrote the journal's final entry—otherwise, she would have noted it. But did she find the seeds?" An idea occurred to her, and she turned to Joseph. "How did Miss Bishop die?"

"We don't know." Joseph's expression was grim. "I was told

that she had a fortnightly delivery of supplies, and one week, the merchant found his previous package had been left, untouched, on the porch. Subsequent searches did not uncover a body, but it was clear that Kensington was deserted. Miss Bishop was never seen again and was eventually declared dead."

Sophie looked back at the letter, and her stomach roiled. It seemed too much of a coincidence that the final journal entry matched the letter's date. Had Miss Bishop gone to retrieve the seeds and met with foul play? E.D.'s letter had been hostile. Surely he wouldn't resort to lure and murder to rid himself of her attention?

Joseph seemed to be thinking along similar lines. He closed the journal, his eyes distant as he stared through the window at the black clouds. "We have two possibilities. Either Miss Bishop found the seeds, or she didn't. If she found them, there is a chance they might be in Kensington. If she didn't, it's possible they're still in town. Though I have no idea what the *odd cow's crooked step* refers to. E.D. seemed concerned that an unintended recipient might take them, which is why he used a code to describe their location. In which case, they're likely to be well hidden."

"Or he could have been lying about having the seeds," Garret growled. He was pacing the room, his shoulders hunched and hands thrust into his pockets. "And even if they exist and we find them, is there any chance they haven't become moist, sprouted, and died in these last hundred years?"

Joseph sighed and turned the letter over. "I wish I had good news, but simply finding the seeds is not enough. E.D. included instructions for their use: '*Soak for one day, then plant in moist soil. Protect the plants from sunlight; they need no more than one or two hours per day—any more, and they will burn. It will take six weeks for them to bloom. Collect the flowers, boil in a small pot of water, and administer to the unwell individual.*'"

"Six weeks!" Garrett spluttered.

Joseph refolded the letter. He looked exhausted, and Sophie was reminded that he'd barely slept the past few days. She took his hand and pressed it, and his lips twitched into something that reminded her of a smile. "I had hoped we would find more immediate assistance in the other volumes," he said, "but their only advice—to destroy the Grimlock's heart—is not an option. We have a choice, then: search for the seeds, praying they are findable, viable, and will help Elise, or seek alternate options."

"What alternate options are there?" Garrett dropped into his chair and ran his hands through his hair. "You yourself had been searching for help during the final months at Northwood, and the only gentleman you found who claimed to have knowledge of the Grimlock died before he even reached us. It feels as though every door we try is locked."

Joseph glanced between his uncle and Sophie. "We should vote. I believe our best chance is in pursuing the seeds."

"Yes." Sophie chewed on her thumb. While the cessant's bloom seemed like a poor hope, it was the only light in an inky night. "I feel as though we should at least look for them. But Elise is your daughter, Garrett—what do you feel?"

He closed his eyes and breathed deeply. "Six weeks...may

heaven have mercy on us. We had better start the hunt for this blasted plant lest we all die of old age before my daughter is cured."

"Then we're agreed." Joseph rose and placed the journal on the desk with the letter on top. "While it's possible they're still in the town, the weather is too foul to leave the house, so I propose we begin our search here."

Garrett nodded as he rose. "Look anywhere a small pouch might fit. That damnable Miss Bishop may have hidden the seeds, too, so keep your eyes peeled for secret compartments and fake drawer bases."

They began their hunt in Miss Bishop's bedroom. Joseph and Sophie went through the cupboard with exacting care, feeling under shelves and pressing on the back wall in case there was a hidden cubbyhole. But the cupboard held no surprises, so they soon moved on to the rest of the room's furniture. Garrett lifted the bed's mattress to allow Joseph to check underneath, and Sophie pulled the drawers out of the writing desk. The room didn't have much furniture, and they exhausted their options in less than an hour. From there, they moved to the adjacent dressing room.

Afternoon had progressed into early evening without Sophie noticing. The natural light was already so poor from the rain that they'd needed lamps for their search, and she didn't realize how late it had become until she looked toward the window and saw nothing but black outside.

They'd missed lunch and were late for dinner. Sophie suggested they pause for food, and Garrett cursed. "I forgot to bring anything to Elise—damn it—wait here, and I'll get something for all of us. Give me a few minutes." He shoved out of the door, and they listened to his footsteps thunder down the stairs.

Joseph had been hunting through a wardrobe of dresses in case the pouch had been left in a pocket, but he closed the doors and turned to Sophie. "It's been a long day. Would you like to rest for a while?"

"Thank you, I'm fine." That wasn't entirely the truth; her back and neck ached, and her head was fuzzy from hunger. But she still had a little adrenaline from the discovery of the secret library and wanted to make as much progress as she could. "I can keep looking until Garrett returns."

Joseph nodded and moved into the washroom on the other side of the dressing room. Sophie returned to the dresses. They had once been very grand; they'd been made out of rich velvets and silks, muslin, and pearls. But the cloth had deteriorated into rags during their century of neglect, and Sophie was forced to hunt for pockets and pouches by touch rather than sight.

Motion caught her attention, and she looked up from her task. A full-length mirror had been set into the door, and although it was tarnished, Sophie could see her own pale face and disheveled hair reflected in it. Something shifted over her shoulder, and she squinted as she tried to make it out.

The shape moved again, and Sophie's heart stuttered with horrible realization: she was staring at the veiled woman.

CHAPTER 16
RESPITE

"JOSEPH...!" THE WORD ESCAPED as a squeak. She could hear her husband shifting through the washroom as he pulled trinkets out of the drawers, but he didn't respond.

The veiled woman loomed closer, creeping out of the gloom that filled the tarnished mirror's surface. Her veil obscured the upper half of her face, but Sophie could easily picture the sharp cheekbones and hollow, proud eyes.

The ink-black dress seemed to gather the shadows around the figure, and when the woman exhaled, a gust of ice-cold air brushed over Sophie's shoulder. Terror caught her in its viselike grip. She opened her mouth to call for Joseph again, but the word died in her throat. The veiled woman stretched a hand forward. Sophie stared in mute horror as long, bony fingers, their knuckles bulging and skin so pale that they looked like bones, reached for her neck.

The lower half of the woman's face contorted as she exposed her teeth in a sneer. They glittered in the pale light, and while it was the only part of her face that Sophie could make out clearly, she could tell that the expression was cruel and angry.

The fingers scratched against Sophie's neck. Their flesh was like winter, and chills spread from the point of contact.

Move! Sophie begged herself. *Scream before it's too late!*

But her body wouldn't obey. She felt paralyzed—trapped—just as she did in the dreams where the Grimlock stalked her through Northwood's bleak halls.

The twitching, wintery fingers tightened around her neck, and the other hand rose up to clasp over her mouth, silencing her, choking off her oxygen.

Something large slammed into the wardrobe behind Sophie. The cold fingers abruptly vanished, and with it, Sophie's capacities were restored. She lurched forward and gasped in a deep breath before turning. Joseph had hit the wardrobe behind where the veiled woman had stood a second before. His eyes were wide, but his hands felt unexpectedly gentle as they fluttered over her throat, checking for bruises. "Are you hurt? Did she hurt you?"

"N-no—" Terror, no longer held at bay by adrenaline, swept through Sophie and pulled the strength from her legs. Before she could collapse, Joseph caught her and pressed her to his chest as he murmured comfort and stroked her hair.

"I'm fine." The words stuck in her throat, so Sophie took a deep breath to steady herself. "Thank you."

Joseph sighed, and she thought she felt him press a kiss to

the top of her head. "You make this so hard," he whispered then asked in a clearer voice, "Why didn't you call me?"

Sophie thought of the unnatural paralysis and squeezed her eyes against the shudders that wanted to run through her. "I couldn't. I tried, but..." She inhaled again, waited until she thought her voice would be steady, then asked, "How did you know?"

"Ha." He kept his hands moving, caressing her back and running over her hair. "You were too quiet. It unnerved me enough that I had to check on you—and I saw that *woman* behind you. That was Miss Bishop, I take it?"

Sophie nodded. Joseph stepped back, his dark eyes scanning her face briefly before he passed his arm about her shoulders and drew her toward the door. "Let's go downstairs. It will be safer there. I hope."

His arm, warm and careful and reassuring, stayed around her as they descended the stairs and followed the mazelike passageways to the back of the house. When they pressed through the large kitchen doors, they found Garrett stirring a gray sludge in a small pot he'd hung over the fireplace. He glanced over his shoulder as they entered. "Hungry, I take it? I hope you like porridge."

"The spirit attacked Sophie." Joseph's voice was soft, but she could feel a barely contained anger roiling under the surface. The tone sent a thrill through her. She didn't meet his eyes but could feel him watching her.

Garrett rose from his crouch and exhaled a lungful of air. "Well, damn."

"We had hoped Miss Bishop would be harmless, but she's not." Joseph pulled a chair out and waited until Sophie sat before removing his coat and draping it about her shoulders. He then rounded the table, poured water into a pot, and set it beside Garrett's in the fire. "She tried to kill Sophie. I feel—and I hope you will both agree with me—that this house is no longer safe enough to stay in alone." He gave Sophie a pointed stare. "We must keep together as much as possible."

Garrett's face was pale. The porridge was boiling violently, but he'd stopped stirring it. "What about Elise? She's harboring the Grimlock. Will Miss Bishop attack her next?"

"I have no idea." Joseph retrieved three cups and laid them on the counter. The familiar scowl darkened his face. "Miss Bishop is supposed to hate the Grimlock. That raises a lot of questions, though. Why hasn't she already attacked Elise, who has lived in this house for nearly two weeks? Why did she seek Sophie out instead?"

Garrett finally took the porridge off the fire and divided it among four bowls. His motions were too clumsy for Sophie to believe his mind was focused on the task. "Is it possible her ghost has no awareness?"

"Like an animal turned too feral to remember its master." Joseph's voice was a murmur. "That was what I'd wondered. Sophie is trying to continue Miss Bishop's work, but perhaps the ghost no longer remembers her life's purpose, only her anger, and is attacking mindlessly. Or perhaps she still has enough of a conscience not to kill a child and is lashing out at the next available target."

The water was also boiling. Joseph wrapped a cloth around the pot's handle, took it to the table, and poured the water into the mugs. Garrett's anxiety hadn't abated but seemed to grow with each second. "I would stay close to Elise all day if I could, but she becomes distressed and aggressive if I try to sit with her for more than a few minutes. But if she's truly at risk—"

"Is that dinner?" The soft voice startled the three of them. They turned and saw Elise standing in the doorway, blinking against the fire's light. Sophie's stomach lurched. The girl looked truly sick; her cheeks were sunken as if she were starving, her black hair hung limp around her shoulders, and her eyes, which had always been tormented and sad, had acquired a dullness that Sophie associated with the chronically ill. But the Grimlock's shining lights no longer haunted the back of them, and the girl was moving and speaking normally.

Garrett held his hand out, and Elise went to him eagerly. "I was about to bring it to you. But you could eat with us tonight if you prefer."

"Yes." Elise smiled. It was a fragile motion but genuine. She settled into the space next to her father, took up the spoon, and began scooping the porridge into her mouth as though it were the first meal she'd had in months.

Joseph rounded the table, placed the cup of tea in front of Sophie, and stroked his fingers across her cheek. "Are you well?"

Sophie clenched her hands so that he wouldn't see her fingers trembling and smiled. "Yes, thank you."

She was surprised by how pleasant that dinner was. Elise

105

finished her bowl in less than a minute, and Garrett cooked more porridge. His earlier frustration had dissolved, and Sophie saw glimpses of the good-humored man she suspected would emerge in a less stressful environment. He joked and laughed heartily as he refilled Elise's bowl multiple times.

Other than her sickliness, Elise showed no symptoms of the Grimlock's habitation. Sophie wondered what that meant. Was the Grimlock only in control sometimes, or had it temporarily released Elise from its grip? Was it, too, concerned about her welfare? If Elise were to die, the Grimlock would no longer have its tether to the mortal realm. *Perhaps this night of respite is insurance—a chance for Elise to regain some of her health.*

Unlike their previous meals, they took their time that night and chatted freely. They all avoided speaking of Kensington or their predicament and talked about mundane topics—the weather, Sophie's city neighbors, animals Garrett had seen living in the forest—and Sophie found herself relaxing properly for the first time since arriving at Kensington. Every few minutes, Joseph stroked her arm, her shoulder, or her hair as though reassuring himself of her presence. She leaned into his touch and even caught him smiling at her.

Eventually even Elise gave up on eating. She rested against her father's shoulder, a contented smile lingering on her lips as her eyelids began to fall. Garrett stroked her hair as he sighed. "I'm tired of searching. Let's have an early night."

Joseph looked at the door leading to the main sections of the house. "I'd be more comfortable if none of us were alone tonight. Perhaps we could carry some blankets and pillows into the parlor."

"Yes, that was what I was thinking. Safety in numbers. Come along, my dear."

CHAPTER 17
THE FOREST

WHEN SOPHIE WOKE, SHE was surprised to find the room lit by a pale golden glow. The clouds had retreated enough to allow some natural sun through the curtains and finally freed them from their perpetual reliance on candles and lamps.

She tilted her head to the side and locked eyes with the portrait hung above the mantel. Miss Bishop's likeness surveyed the parlor, seeming to assess and judge the disarray her unwanted guests had forced on the musty room.

When they'd retired the night before, the men had insisted Sophie take one chaise longue and had given the second to Elise while they slept on the floor. Joseph now sat beside the head of Sophie's makeshift bed, arms crossed and long legs folded. He gave her a wan smile when he saw she was awake.

"Where's Elise?" Sophie shifted to sit up and tried to push her hair away from her face. It had come free from its braid during the night and tickled her cheeks and neck.

"Gone." Joseph rocked forward, rose, and crossed to the fireplace. He took a plate from the mantel then sat beside Sophie and offered her the dish, which held a light breakfast. "Garrett and I had intended to take turns keeping watch last night, but we both fell asleep, I'm afraid. Elise disappeared during the early morning. She is not in her room. Garrett is searching for her, though he says he doesn't have much hope of finding her. She's been lost and reappeared repeatedly over the last few weeks."

"Oh." Sophie didn't feel hungry, but she nibbled at the crackers. She hadn't fooled herself into thinking Elise's awareness would be permanent, but she'd hoped it would last longer than it had. *Six weeks!* Garrett's sentiments echoed in her mind, and she found herself agreeing with him. Six weeks felt like a lifetime when Elise was suffering so severely. And that period of time would only start when—*if*—they found the seeds.

The food turned to dust in her mouth, and she dropped the remaining cracker back onto the plate.

"Don't despair." Joseph's voice was soft as he extended his hand to help her rise. She had the distinct impression that, during the hours he'd sat awake the night before, he'd followed the same mental process that she'd just gone through. "Come, let's take an hour or two for ourselves before resuming the search. You'll feel better once you've washed and eaten. If you like, we can take a walk outside now that the rain has cleared."

Sophie opened her mouth to refuse the break, but then her eyes drifted back to Miss Bishop's painting. The severe, angular face seemed to watch over the room with mixed disdain and pride. The furniture in the room had once been so grand but was now smotheringly dilapidated. The once-red curtains were light-faded rags, the threads of the carpet scuffed up when she kicked her feet against it, and every corner held an abundance of dust and cobwebs. She realized how desperately she wanted to escape the house even if just for half an hour. "That would be lovely."

Joseph seemed intent on making sure she wasn't left alone. He turned his back but didn't leave the room while she washed and changed. Despite her protests, he urged her to eat breakfast before they left, and accompanied her to fetch a shawl and boots before they ventured outdoors.

Kensington's front doors, not touched since Joseph and Sophie's arrival, groaned painfully as they opened. Sophie blinked against the unexpectedly bright light as they stepped through the grand arch then inhaled a lungful of the fresh, chilled air before taking Joseph's arm. Her husband hooked a loaded hunting rifle over the other then led her down the front steps and into what remained of the garden.

The rain had washed up many dead plants and tipped over two of the marble statues. The ground had dried a little overnight, but Sophie's feet still sank into mud, and she was glad for her thick boots. The sun was bright, and the air tasted crisper than it did in the musty hallways and cloistered rooms. The morning was frigid. Sophie shivered despite the coat and shawl, but her sense of relief at being outside of Kensington's crumbling walls was immense.

"Where to?" Joseph asked, his breath pluming when he

spoke. Even he seemed to have brightened under the influence of the outdoors. "Would you like to see the back garden or explore the forest?"

If the indistinct views she'd glimpsed through the windows were accurate, the back garden would be as depressingly dead as the front. Sophie longed to be among life and health, so she nodded toward the trees. "The forest!"

The spongy ground squelched under their feet as they crossed the front yard but improved as they moved onto the grassy area beyond. They approached the forest's edge and began walking parallel to it. That section of the woods was dense and dim and still wet from the rain. Joseph said there were supposed to be paths through the woods, though, so they set out in search of them.

Bracken crunched under their feet, and tiny insects darted out of their path. The forest was alive with sound; hidden under the gentle rushing noise of leaves rubbing against each other and the patter of rain being shaken loose from the boughs was a symphony of birdcalls and insect chatter. Joseph didn't speak, but he was smiling, clearly enjoying being near woods again. Sophie couldn't contain her own grin. *Perhaps he prefers the country to the city after all.*

As they followed the curve of the wood's edge, Sophie's attention was drawn to some dirty white pebbles poking out of the ground ahead. She thought they might be the beginning of a path, but as she strolled closer, she realized some of the shapes were too large for that purpose.

Joseph stopped walking and placed one hand on Sophie's shoulder to halt her as well. Caution flooded back into his previously relaxed pose as he squinted at the rocks. "I think we had better go back inside, my dear."

"What is it?" Sophie took a step closer despite Joseph's hand and gasped.

A human skull, half-buried, leered at them. A little below it, a long bone—a femur, Sophie guessed—poked out of the dirt.

"Oh." Sophie stepped back and tightened her grip on Joseph's arm. She swallowed against the queasiness that rose, and she tried to breathe evenly.

"Come," Joseph murmured and tried to pull her back, but Sophie couldn't take her eyes off the bones.

"They must have been unearthed during the rain," she mumbled. "It—it did the same to the garden's plants—"

A thought, almost like premonition, struck her, and she turned to look at the house. "Joseph, those windows up there—does one of them belong to Miss Bishop's bedroom?"

Joseph tilted his head to one side. "Yes. Yes, it should be that room on the second floor, partway along."

"Oh." Sophie turned back to the bones. "I think I saw her here last night. When I called for you, remember? I'd seen Miss Bishop standing near the edge of the forest. She'd been staring at something on the ground. I think…I think this might be her grave."

CHAPTER 18
A SHALLOW GRAVE

"YOU'RE CERTAIN?" GARRETT LEANED forward on the kitchen table, hands clasped around a cup of coffee. "It wouldn't be, say, a servant, or another family member?"

"It could be, of course." Joseph sat opposite his uncle with Sophie nestled at his side. "But there are clues suggesting it is truly Miss Bishop."

He kept one hand on Sophie's, his thumb strumming her knuckles. The touch warmed her far more than the hot drink— almost as much as it filled her with confusion. Joseph's attitude toward her had changed. Had he really been that impressed by her discovery of the library, or had she said or done something to rekindle his feelings? As much as she wanted to understand the alteration, Sophie was forced to put those thoughts aside for later examination. Their present situation was more pressing.

"Clues?" Garrett looked haggard, and Sophie doubted he'd

slept much, but his eyes were lit with curiosity as they darted between his companions.

"First, the bones are old. But their condition is too good for them to have lain there much more than a century. The timing matches Miss Bishop's death."

"That's hardly conclusive evidence."

"Be patient; there's more. The grave is shallow. A hundred years of erosion and two days of heavy rain were enough to unearth the body. That suggests it was buried unofficially. Possibly by just one person." Joseph raised his eyebrows meaningfully. "Her only remaining companion, for example—the elderly Mr. Trent. He would have loved her dearly enough to bury her but may have lacked the strength to dig a deep grave."

Garrett shrugged. "Or it could be a servant no one particularly cared for."

"Servants likely would have been taken to town and buried in the public cemetery there. What gentlewoman wants a grave within view of the master bedroom unless there is an attachment to the occupant?"

"Especially since it was marked," Sophie added. "It may not have a proper gravestone, but a rock was placed a little above the skull."

Garrett snorted. "I didn't expect you to be so enthusiastic about this, my dear."

Sophie felt herself turn pink but didn't retreat. "Do you see what it means, though? If it's Miss Bishop—and I'm certain it is—this could explain why her spirit lingers on earth."

"Her grave has been disturbed," Joseph said. "Her bones are exposed to the elements. It's ignoble, and I know it would chagrin a woman as proud and proper as Miss Bishop appears to have been."

Garrett's eyebrows rose. He seemed to finally understand why they were so excited about the discovery. "Ah—and you think—"

"If we were to rebury her—in a proper, deep grave—it might allow her spirit to be at rest."

Garrett slammed his cup onto the table so abruptly that Sophie jumped. "I'll get the shovels." He pushed out of his chair.

Sophie and Joseph followed their uncle out of the kitchen and into the dining room, littered with travel cases. By the time they caught up, he was already digging through a large trunk. Sophie glimpsed rope and metal tools.

"How did you bring all of this here?" she asked in wonderment.

Garrett snorted as he retrieved two shovels and a trowel. "With a second carriage and a cart. I didn't know what we would find when we arrived or how long we were likely to stay, and I packed as much as I could." He crossed to another case and dug through a swath of fabric before retrieving two sets of leather riding gloves. He wrinkled his nose as he passed one pair to Joseph. "Digging through dirt will ruin these, but it's better than leaving our hands uncovered."

Sophie glanced between them. "Did you bring a third pair, by any chance?"

Joseph shot her a hard look. "You should stay inside."

"It's safer if we stay together," Sophie countered. "And I'd like to help if I can. I'm not squeamish."

"Ha!" Garret grinned as he turned back to the trunk. "You found yourself a spark of a woman, didn't you, Joseph?"

Joseph exhaled, but there was a hint of fondness in his eyes. "Yes, I certainly did."

Garrett dug a third pair of gloves out of the case and threw them to Sophie. They were far too large for her, but she pulled them on and balled her hands into fists so that they wouldn't fall off as she returned outside with the men.

The day had warmed enough that Sophie no longer shivered as they crossed the lawn. The ground was gradually drying, though deep puddles lingered wherever there was a crevice or indentation in the ground.

They slowed as they neared the exposed bones, and the significance of what they were about to do crashed over Sophie. Her first encounter with a dead body had been in Northwood, and it had been so brief and so clouded by fear and panic that she hadn't been fully sensible of the experience. This time, however, there was no shirking the platter of mortality laid before them.

The skull's jaw hung open, missing many of its teeth and tilted at an odd angle. Farther down, the pelvis bone jutted from the earth. Shreds of fabric still clung to the white shape, though they were so badly decayed that Sophie couldn't guess what part of the dress they had belonged to. The femur had drifted away from the body in the century since it had been laid to rest. It poked out to one side, seeming to make a mockery of the burial.

Sophie swallowed and found her throat was tight. It was easy to view the bones with repulsion, but they had once belonged to a human filled with many of the same fears, ideas, and hopes that Sophie held. Miss Bishop's ghost might be cruel, but that didn't mean the living woman had been void of good traits. *She dedicated her life to ridding Northwood of the Grimlock. Joseph says she wrote to her brother often. She didn't abandon her home even after the village died. And she loved a man.*

Sophie glanced toward her husband. He'd shed his coat and worked beside Garrett, digging up clumps of the soft earth as they created Miss Bishop's new grave.

How would I feel if these bones belonged to Joseph? I would want them treated kindly. Respectfully. I would want his spirit to be at rest. Miss Bishop deserves that too, no matter how vengeful her ghost has become. She deserves peace.

Sophie picked up the trowel, knelt beside the bones, and began easing them out of the earth. Joseph stopped his digging to watch her. Surprise flashed over his countenance, but he didn't interrupt or stop her. He returned to his own task after a moment.

Freeing the bones was slow, laborious work. They were fragile and cracked easily. Eventually, Sophie discovered it was easier if she exhumed the dirt around them too. Each time she retrieved a bone, she set it to one side, arranging it as carefully and respectfully as she could.

Near the end of her work, when all of the large bones had been salvaged and Sophie was focused on finding as many of the smaller fragments as she could, Joseph knelt beside her.

"How do you feel?"

"Fine, thank you." She was a little surprised to realize that was the truth. The bones had horrified her when they'd first discovered them, but she no longer found them repulsive. "I think I've retrieved most of them."

"We've finished the grave. It's close to six feet deep; nothing short of an earthquake will disturb her rest there."

Sophie nodded and rose to her feet. Dirt caked the gloves, her dress was marred by grass stains, and strands of hair had come free from the bun. She was cleaner than Joseph, though; it would be a mammoth task to purge the mud from his clothes.

The base of the new grave had filled with water. They briefly debated how to bury Miss Bishop. It seemed crude and insulting to simply throw the bones into the hole, but the grave was too deep to lower them in by hand. At last, Garrett fetched a clean sheet from the house, on which they arranged the bones as close to their proper order as they could. Then Joseph and Garrett each took two of the sheet's corners, knelt at opposite ends of the grave, and lowered Miss Bishop into her new burial place. Once her body came to rest on the ground, they flipped the ends of the sheet over her in a makeshift shroud.

"Ready?" Joseph asked Garrett as he picked up his shovel.

"Oh! Can we wait a moment?" An idea had occurred to Sophie, and she hurried to the forest's edge. Small wildflowers dotted the spaces between the trees where they'd been sheltered from the rain, and she gathered a bundle and tied them together with a strip of long grass. She returned to the grave and released the spray into it, letting it fall onto the shroud.

Joseph and Garrett took up their shovels and began returning the earth to the hole. Sophie stood back, hands clasped, and said a silent prayer for the dead woman. She then lifted her eyes to Kensington. The grand building reminded her a little of its owner—proud and strong but diminished and damaged by age. The building's left wing lay in rubble, and the windows were lifeless and broken.

A curtain twitched, and Sophie strained to see who was inside the room. *Elise? No—she's too tall—*

Miss Bishop, barely visible through the shadows, stood in the window, chin held high as she watched her bones being returned to the earth. Then the curtains fell back into place, and the woman disappeared from sight.

"There." Joseph, breathing heavily and with sweat creating tracks through his dirt-smudged face, stepped back from the grave. The dirt had been packed into it neatly, leaving a human-sized rectangle of bare ground. "Garrett, do you think we can move the gravestone?"

Garrett snorted. "It's a rock, not a gravestone. Doesn't look too big, though. Let's give it a try."

It took a minute, but they managed to dig the stone out of the ground and move it to sit at the head of the new grave. They all took a step back and lingered a moment then turned and retraced their steps to Kensington.

I'm glad we could do that. Sophie found Joseph's hand. They both still wore their gloves, but he squeezed in response to her touch and gave her a gentle smile. *Even if her spirit hadn't been haunting this home, she deserved a proper burial.*

They reentered Kensington. During their work, clouds had gathered over the afternoon sun, and the house was unnaturally dim. Returning to the ancient building was like stepping back into a bad dream. Their footsteps echoed off the foyer's cracked marble, and it was easy to taste how stale and lifeless the air was inside the building.

Joseph and Garrett placed their dirty gloves and coats on a sideboard while Sophie waited. "We'd better fetch some water, clean up, and change," Joseph said. "Sophie, would you mind sitting in the next room? My hope is that Miss Bishop's spirit will be at peace, but I'd rather take precautions until we're certain."

Sophie's answer died before it could reach her lips. Movement at the top of the stairs had drawn her notice, and she felt her heart flutter at the sight of the figure standing there.

The sun, angled over the opposite side of the house, was unable to dispel the shadows that obscured the tall, straight-backed woman.

Miss Bishop's veil hung over the top half of her face, hiding her expression, but her pose felt hostile. She held impeccably still, skeletal hands gripping a large, long shape, her head inclined toward Sophie. As she shifted, a glint of faint light reflected off the object she held. *An ax,* Sophie realized with a swell of horror. *Why is she carrying an ax?*

"*Ha.*" The corpse exhaled the single note of mirth. It was a cracked, distorted noise, something that should have never been voiced in the mortal realm. Her head tilted, and her bloodless lips stretched into a manic grimace of delight.

"Watch out!" Joseph yelled at the same instant Sophie became aware of a groaning above her. She tilted her head back to look at the ceiling and saw the grand chandelier, its iron brackets resplendent in a swath of cobwebs, shudder.

She only had a fraction of a second to realize the metal chain holding the chandelier to the roof had been damaged, then the metal gave way, and the wrought-iron monstrosity plunged toward her.

There was no time to move. No time to draw breath.

Then Joseph slammed into her, pushing her out of the chandelier's path. She fell to the ground, jarred and shaken, her world a blur of motion and dizziness. The metal wailed as it collided with the marble floor.

Joseph screamed. It was an agonized, broken sound that collapsed into silence before Sophie could turn.

From across the room Garrett yelled, "No!"

"Joseph!" Still winded from the fall, Sophie was only able to exhale the word as a terrified gasp. "Joseph!"

CHAPTER 19
DIVIDED

THE INSIDE OF SOPHIE'S chest felt raw, as though someone had dragged a pumice stone across her most sensitive organs. Her heart ached, and her eyes burned, but she wouldn't allow herself to cry. *Now is not the time to be weak.*

Her fears—the very anxieties that had pushed her to accompany Joseph to Kensington—had been realized. She'd come to keep him safe, but her presence had only brought him harm.

Joseph lay on the chaise longue in the parlor. He was sheet white and his breathing shallow. Garrett knelt at his side, tight lipped and gaunt, his hands still caked with blood from where he'd bandaged his nephew's leg.

Sophie had tried to help, but her hands had shaken too badly to be any use, so Garrett had told her to talk to Joseph and keep him conscious instead. She knelt beside his head, stroking his black hair and murmuring anything kind that came into her mind. Joseph's eyes were closed, but his expression was tight, and she couldn't tell if he was still awake.

Her gaze drifted back to his leg. From the foot to midthigh was a swath of bandages. Crimson patches appeared in the white cloth and grew larger with each passing minute.

He's going to lose the leg. The phrase, spoken in her uncle's voice, echoed through Sophie's mind. Her uncle, a hardworking physician who had catered to merchants and those gentry who couldn't afford the expensive doctors, had spoken the words one morning when Sophie and her father had visited him. He'd been saying goodbye to a patient when they'd arrived, and, as he'd closed the door behind them, her uncle had casually voiced the phrase that would haunt her. *He's going to lose the leg.*

That man's injury had been nowhere near as severe as Joseph's. Sophie squeezed her eyes closed as she ran her fingers over her husband's forehead, brushing the thick hair back and murmuring anything she could think of. "It's going to be all right. You'll be fine. It's going to be all right."

If we have to lose his leg, please, Lord, let that be all. I couldn't survive losing the rest of him too.

"Could you stay alone for an hour or two?"

Garrett's gravelly voice startled Sophie. She lifted her head and saw the older man frowning at his blood-caked hands.

"I-I—"

"There's a plant that would help close the wounds and keep them clean. It sometimes grows in this sort of forest. I want to look for it if you think you would be safe here alone."

"Of course." Sophie sat straighter, relieved to have a course of action. "I can help look too—"

"No. It would be too risky. Stay with Joseph."

Sophie looked back at her husband. His expression was still tight, but his breathing had become even, telling her he was asleep at last. She nodded.

Garrett rolled to his feet and left without another word. Sophie waited to hear the front door open and close, but it didn't. Instead, Garrett reentered the parlor after a moment. He laid two objects onto the floor beside Sophie. "As a precaution." He gave her shoulder a brief squeeze and left. This time she heard the great door close as Garrett set out for the forest.

Sophie looked at the objects she'd been given: a pistol and a long, wicked-looking knife. She exhaled and inclined her head to kiss Joseph's cheek. He didn't stir.

Why is she so angry? Sophie couldn't shake the memory of the woman who'd stood in the shadows at the top of the stairs and the way she'd laughed as she watched them. *I wish we'd never buried her. I'd thought everyone deserved rest after death, but I was wrong. She deserves to have her bones laid bare and picked at by birds for eternity, the hateful, hideous woman.*

Sophie wiped the tears off her cheeks, her hands shaking with mingled anger and grief. She'd never felt their isolation as acutely as she did at that moment. There was no way to get Joseph to a doctor until the carriage returned. Even then, it was nearly a full day's trip to the nearest town—a tiny village that held almost nothing except an inn and a pub. *What sort of care would he get there?*

Joseph shifted and grimaced. Sophie returned to stroking his hair, murmuring gentle words, and his expression softened again.

Kensington's front door groaned as it opened, and Sophie turned expectantly. *That was faster than I expected. Did he find the plant he needs?*

No one entered the parlor, though, and Sophie couldn't hear any footsteps. She rose, crossed to the doorway, and looked into the foyer. It was empty.

"Garrett?"

No answer.

The hairs rose on the back of her arms. She shivered and backed into the parlor, glancing over the room, assessing each shadowed crevice and dim corner with fresh wariness.

Miss Bishop's portrait seemed to watch her, the gray eyes catching the insipid light coming through the window.

The window——! There's someone outside!

Sophie's heart was a quick, harsh drum in her chest as she crossed to the glass. Age and accumulated dirt had made the panes smoky, and two of them were cracked. She leaned forward until her nose was an inch from the glass and squinted though it.

A figure moved across the open, grassy expanse, heading toward the woods. Sophie inhaled sharply. She recognized Elise's black dress and hair.

Where has she been? And where is she going? Into the forest? No——

The girl was moving toward the gap in the trees that led to the overgrown path and decayed bridge.

Anxiety rose through Sophie like a wave, flaring the ache in her chest. She turned to look at Joseph, who was still unconscious and too injured to move. Garrett was somewhere in the forest, but she didn't even know which direction he'd taken.

I have to bring her back. Sophie pushed away from the window then stopped. *No, it would be insanity to follow her. Remember, that's not Elise—it's the Grimlock.*

She squeezed her eyes closed and shook her head. *It's still Elise. She may not be in control, but she's still inside her body, and she needs help. Joseph would follow her. And I should too.*

She snatched the pistol and the knife off the floor then placed the former in her left pocket and wrapped the latter's blade in her handkerchief before carefully sliding it into the right pocket.

Joseph shifted, his brow contracting, and she crossed to him and kissed his cheek tenderly. "I'll be back soon," she whispered. Her heart ached for him; she hoped he wouldn't wake while he was alone. "Be safe."

Then she ran through the parlor door and crossed the foyer. The front door still stood open a crack from where Elise had exited. Sophie slipped through and blinked against the dim outside light. The rain clouds had returned, though they only spat small specks onto the garden, which was still recovering from the earlier onslaught.

Sophie inhaled deeply, filling her lungs with the cold air, then picked up her skirts and ran after the girl who was already disappearing between the trees.

CHAPTER 20
WINDOWS LIKE EYES

SOPHIE HAD TRIED TO pack sensibly, choosing light, comfortable dresses that would allow her to move freely, but she was still hampered by their bulk. By the time she reached the forest's edge, she was panting. The light rain left a cold sheen over her face and stuck strands of hair to her forehead and neck. She'd tried calling Garrett's name several times as she'd neared the edge of the forest, hoping that he might still be close enough to hear her, but no voice replied. She would have to follow and somehow retrieve the girl alone.

Sophie had to slow her pace to a half run as she entered the woods. Tree roots and overturned rocks crisscrossed the path, threatening to trip her or break an ankle if she rushed.

Elise had been moving quickly. Sophie didn't know what the girl's goal was but hoped she would stay on the path long enough for Sophie to catch up. Elise's timing had been impeccable; she'd left the house minutes after her father, safe in the knowledge that neither Garrett nor Joseph would pursue her. Perhaps she'd hoped Sophie would be too frightened to take any action on her own.

I might have been wiser if I had *been too frightened,* Sophie thought wryly as she ducked under a low branch.

As she moved deeper into the woods, the forest's cacophony seemed to swell. The scratching rustle of leaves, insects chirruping, and even the crunch of small animals digging through the underbrush surrounded her. The air was dense and humid, seeming to stick in Sophie's throat and making it difficult to breathe.

She pushed on, fighting to maintain her pace despite the sensation that she was suffocating. The path was winding and so overgrown in places that Sophie had to slow down and hunt for the infrequent white rocks to be certain of the correct direction.

At last, when the walk had become so long that Sophie was starting to worry she was lost after all, the trees thinned and released her into the clearing that overlooked the chasm.

A deep, prolonged, muted roar reached her. Sophie circled closer to the cliff's edge—so close that sweat slicked her palms and her chest constricted with quiet panic—and saw that the small river had been engorged by the rains and turned into a rushing, tumultuous, frothing torrent.

She took three steps back and breathed deeply, refilling her starved lungs with oxygen.

Did Elise cross the bridge?

There were no signs of the child, but Sophie's intuition told her over the bridge was the right direction to go. There was nowhere else to turn unless Elise had left the path and entered the forest—in which case it would be nearly impossible to find her.

The wood-and-rope bridge shuddered in the breeze, and Sophie's courage came dangerously close to failing her. Crossing it the first time had been terrifying, but at least then she'd had Joseph to beckon her forward.

She went to the bridge's opening and placed her foot on the first slat. It groaned. The rains had made it slimy, and Sophie had to grip the ropes on either side before she trusted her footing enough to take a second step.

The bridge swung under her movement, its ropes groaning as they strained. Bile rose in her throat. She kept her eyes focused on the chasm's other side, refusing to glance at the rushing waters below.

Step by step, she inched forward, knowing that if she stopped moving, fear would freeze her in place. She reached the halfway point. The bridge rocked, swinging her in dizzying arcs, seeming determined to pitch her over the sides. Hot tears stung her cheeks, but she didn't dare lift her hands from where they hovered above the ropes. She took another step.

The slat broke with a sickening crack. Sophie's foot plunged through it, and she shrieked, grabbing for the ropes, for the intact boards, her hands grasping for purchase anywhere she could find it. She felt as though she were already plunging into the gorge, but when she opened her eyes, she found she was still crouched on the bridge.

She kept still for a long moment as she waited for the bridge's careening to slow, then she eased her leg back through the hole with great care. Her boots had been high enough and strong enough to protect her from being cut by the fractured wood, but aches along the side of her calf told her it would be bruised the next day.

Her legs shook horribly as she made them take her weight. Caution hadn't been able to protect her from the breaking wood, so fear pushed her to be reckless and to race forward as though the bridge were becoming more dangerous with every moment she spent on it. The opposite side drew nearer—now ten paces away, now just five—and at last she collapsed to her knees on solid, steady ground.

Sophie allowed herself a minute to breathe deeply and get her shaking under control. She wanted to take longer, but she knew every second she waited would increase the risk that she wouldn't catch up to Elise at all. She was dizzy and light-headed when she regained her feet, but the path ahead—the one their coach had come through—was wider and straighter than the one leading to Kensington, and she was soon able to increase her pace to a brisk jog.

She glanced to either side as she ran, hoping to find some trace of Elise—a scrap of cloth snagged on a branch, or maybe even the girl herself hiding among the trees—but the path could have lain empty for the last century for all the signs of life she found.

At last, the trees opened into a clear patch of grass. The ground sloped down ahead of her, leading toward the dead town's center, which was submerged in a layer of mist. Farther away, farms, long abandoned and barren, stretched for kilometers before the land was swallowed back into the forest.

Sophie paused there and used the high ground's advantage to look for any motion or color among the shops and houses. What had been a sprinkle earlier was growing into a slow drizzle, obfuscating the view and blurring the town's shapes, and she kept having to wipe the rain out of her eyes.

A flicker of movement came from near the town's center. Sophie squinted, but the motion didn't repeat itself. *It could be a bird. Maybe a shop sign that moved in the wind. Or it might be Elise.*

She set out in its direction, walking quickly but with her eyes skipping over the gray roofs and bleached walls.

The town wasn't large. The main street ran through it like a backbone with narrower roads leading off it like contorted ribs. The town's center had been dedicated to shops, inns, and a large, mostly collapsed meeting hall. The lesser streets held houses and some smaller shops. Sophie glanced through the windows as she passed them. She couldn't believe how much furniture had been abandoned. Tables, benches, chairs, cabinets, even a piano—anything too large or heavy to transport easily had been resigned to neglect and decay. Perhaps their owners had hoped to one day return for them, but the pieces of furniture were now crumbling under a coating of dust and the mats of cobwebs from long-deceased spiders.

She shuddered. The rain was seeping through her dress and

chilling her. The mist swirled around her as she walked through it, and the town seemed eerily, unnaturally quiet.

Then the silence was broken by a small keening sound. Sophie halted. She slipped her hand into the pocket with the pistol and fastened her fingers around its grip. Then, her breathing quick, she began to slink forward. The sound was quiet and pitiable but echoed through the buildings in such a way that Sophie felt it was coming from all about her.

She sucked in a sharp breath. A swirl of mist had shifted, giving her a glimpse of a figure in the distance, so faint that it looked like a wraith among the gray buildings. It was rocking rhythmically. The motion was so eerie that Sophie had to fight the urge to run. Instead, teeth clenched so tightly that they ached, every nerve in her body quivering, Sophie stepped forward, closer to the figure, close enough to see—

"Elise," she breathed and sprinted forward.

The girl sat on an inn's doorstep, arms folded around her torso, as she cried. Her eyelids were red and puffy and her nose tinged pink from the cold. In the pale light and with her wet hair plastered over her face, she looked ghastly. She raised her head as Sophie approached, and relief flashed over her features. "Sophie! What happened? Where am I?"

"In town." There were no lights in the child's eyes, so Sophie sat on the step next to her and passed an arm around her shoulders, trying to warm her and protect her from the rain. "The one we passed through to reach Kensington. Do you remember it?"

Elise shook her head, causing drops of water to spray from

her hair. "I d-don't remember much. At all. I know we've been in Kensington for two or three days, but I can't recall arriving."

"Oh." Sophie licked her lips, trying to find a way to phrase her words gently. "You...you've been here for more than a few days. You and your father arrived over a fortnight ago. Joseph and I came three days past."

Elise took the news more stoically than Sophie had expected. She raised her head, blinked back tears, and swallowed. "I see."

She doesn't remember anything of her time under the Grimlock's control. That's a mercy in a way, but it must be terrifying for her.

"Do you remember why you came into town?" Sophie knew she needed to return them both to Kensington quickly, but she sensed it was important to find out why the Grimlock had led his small charge to town then abandoned her there. "Where were you when you...woke up?"

"Sitting here." Elise offered a crumpled, damp piece of paper to Sophie. "I was holding this. I couldn't remember where I was or how to get home, but I can feel that he's angry. Something went wrong."

Sophie took the paper and unfolded it. It was old and disintegrating, and the ink had bled badly in the rain, but Sophie still recognized the quick, messy hand. *Miss Bishop, once again, I must insistently refuse your request for a meeting...*

It was the letter from E.D. that detailed where he'd hidden the cessant's bloom seeds. Elise—*the Grimlock*, Sophie corrected herself—must have found it and come in search of the plant.

Sophie quickly reread the letter's bewildering directions. *I have left a pouch containing three seeds hidden in the secret nest under the odd cow's crooked step.* She raised her head. They were sitting on the stoop of a decrepit inn. On the hinged wooden sign above them, the words "The Spotted Horse" were barely legible. Below that was a drawing that must have been intended to look like a prancing horse but had been rendered so poorly that it was more like a misshapen blob. *It looks a little like a cow,* Sophie realized with a thrill of excitement.

She looked back at their feet. The stone steps must have once been balanced neatly but now lay in disarray. The second step's corner had chipped away to reveal a small cubbyhole underneath. *A secret nest.* Sophie dropped to her knees and reached into the hole, feeling around carefully, her fingers running over a century of grime but without finding any parcel. She sat back, disappointed but not surprised. Elise said the Grimlock was angry. *He came here to find the seeds, but they were already gone.*

Elise watched her curiously. She still sniffled occasionally, but her voice was steady when she asked, "Are you looking for something? Is that why we're staying here?"

"Yes," Sophie said, dropping back onto the step and trying to rub strands of wet hair out of her face without transferring any of the grime from her fingers. "This lets us exclude one location from our search, but there are still many places to look." *So many.* Sophie cast her mind over Kensington—it had hundreds of rooms with the potential for dozens of hidden pockets and no guarantee that the seeds would be found in them. Despair threatened to submerge her again, but she smiled for Elise's sake.

"Your father is a stubborn man, though, and I'm sure he's not going to give up until he finds a solution."

Elise's black eyes were fixed on her boots. She still looked ghastly, but the corners of her mouth twitched up. "I'm glad we came here to look for something. I thought—I was afraid—"

"You can tell me."

"I thought he might have taken me here so that I couldn't harm anyone. I know the monster is using me. I was worried I might have attacked people—*hurt* people—and he brought me here so that I couldn't anymore."

It was a chilling thought and brought a reminder of how precarious Sophie's position was, sitting beside the child when the Grimlock could seize control at any moment. She pushed the thought from her mind, gave Elise's shoulder a gentle press, and rose. "We had better get home. I'm freezing, and I'm sure you must be too. And if your father comes back and finds us gone—"

She broke off as a clatter sounded from farther down the street. Both Sophie and Elise turned, squinting through the rain and fog, toward the source of the noise. For a moment, Sophie struggled to differentiate the assembly of gray shapes through the mist. There was a post poking out of the mud, a crumbling sign, the outline of a bank, an open doorway…and *in* that doorway was…

She sucked in a sharp breath and felt for Elise blindly. Her fingers fixed over the girl's sleeve, and she tugged her backward, away from the tall figure that stood in the shadowed entrance and watched them with empty eyes.

CHAPTER 21
THE RESURRECTED

"RUN," SOPHIE WHISPERED, NOT daring to raise her voice as she watched the figure in the doorway opposite. She reached into her pocket and pulled the pistol out. "Follow the pathway to the top of the hill, through the forest, and across the bridge. I'll follow. *Run.*"

Elise's wide, terrified eyes locked on Sophie for a second, then she turned and dashed into the mist, her footfalls so light that they faded from hearing within seconds.

Sophie began backing away from the shadowed figure as she raised the pistol toward its face. The corpse's dried skin stretched tight over its features, its lips shrank back from yellowed teeth, and strands of gray hair hung about its sunken cheeks. Rags clung to the gaunt figure. It held perfectly still, its attention fixed on Sophie with the intensity of a cat preparing to pounce on a mouse.

It's exactly like those creatures that lived around Northwood's perimeter—reanimated corpses bent to the Grimlock's will. The monster's presence must have woken it.

A floorboard creaked behind Sophie. She gasped and leaped to one side, turning in the same motion, and found a second corpse standing in the inn's doorway. It had suffered the same decaying effects as its partner, and standing barely an arm's length away, Sophie could see the oozing cracks as well as puckers and unnatural bulges in its skin and hear the rattling breath as it exhaled.

Sophie swallowed, stepping back cautiously, scarcely daring to breathe. Her hands shook so badly that she didn't know if she would be able to fire the gun. *They might not hold any animosity toward us. The Grimlock raised them, but that doesn't mean it controls them—*

The corpse's face contorted into a snarl. Sophie had a second's warning as the cadaver crouched, then it was leaping toward her, scabbed fingers outstretched, jaw stretched wide.

The gun's crack was deafening. Bone fragments sprayed over Sophie, stinging her face as they glanced off, and the now-headless figure collapsed.

Sophie stifled a shriek as she stumbled away. She couldn't take her eyes off the body, terrified that it might begin to claw itself upright, lifting the headless neck and stretching its unnaturally thin arms toward her once more, but it lay still and lifeless in the mud.

A rattling breath came from behind her, and a door on her

other side creaked as it opened. Sophie, dreading what she would see, raised her gaze from the cadaver.

More figures were emerging from the fog, slicked wet from the splatters of rain, their attention fixed on her. She counted more than a dozen of them—too many for the five bullets remaining in her gun. Terrified nausea welled in her stomach.

How many dead were laid to rest in this town? How full was the graveyard? Did the Grimlock raise them all?

A scream pierced the air. It was high and tight and sent tremors of panic through Sophie's bones. *Elise.*

Dread for the girl she'd sent into the mist spurred her to movement. She turned and ran, her breathing rough and her wet skirts tangling around her ankles as she raced through the town's backbone and toward the hill.

The dead launched themselves after her. Sophie's ears filled with the sounds of a hundred feet matching her pace and the muted crackles of a hundred long-dried lungs billowing. She didn't allow herself the luxury of glancing over her shoulder, but she could feel the cadavers close behind, their bony fingers grasping toward her.

Mist swirled at the top of the hill. As Sophie gained the slope, she saw Elise struggling with two corpses. Sophie raised her gun but didn't dare fire. Elise was tangled with the figures, twisting and kicking, and any bullets would be just as likely to hit the girl as her attackers.

Elise's boot smashed into one of the creatures' face, and its head snapped back with a sickening crunch. She rolled away from the second corpse, which bought Sophie enough space to aim the gun and fire.

The shot clipped the figure's shoulder. The impact caused it to reel. Sophie stretched her hand to Elise to pull her up. "Run! Across the bridge!"

Elise gained her feet. Sophie fired two blind shots over her shoulder as they dashed into the forest. Her lungs burned, but fear kept her legs moving. Crashing noises blended into the thundering footfalls as the corpses spread through the woods. Elise, lithe and quick, matched Sophie's pace easily, moving like a wraith at her side.

They burst out of the woods and into the glade facing the chasm. There was no time to pause—no time to be afraid of the bridge or to worry if it would carry two people at once or to care about whether the wooden slats were going to break. They dashed across its length, clutching at the rope railing when their feet threatened to slip out from under them, doing their best to balance as the bridge lurched and rocked.

A gunshot made Sophie flinch. She looked up and saw a figure among the trees. The posture was strikingly familiar. *It couldn't be—he was too badly hurt—*

Joseph re-aimed his rifle and fired again. The bridge shuddered as one of the living dead was felled.

"Keep your head down!" Sophie placed her hand on Elise's hair and nudged her so that they ran doubled over. The edge of the bridge was only feet away. Sophie could feel the structure straining as more of the cadavers spilled onto the narrow pass. The ropes were stretched tight, the tension palpable, and Sophie's attention fixed on the wooden supports anchored into the ground.

A second figure—Garrett—emerged from the trees and raised his own rifle to join Joseph's fire.

Elise left the bridge first, followed by Sophie a second later. The girl kept running, aiming for her father and the safety he offered, but Sophie dropped to her knees at the bridge's entrance and pulled the knife out of her left pocket.

There were too many corpses to fight. When she glanced at the bridge's length, she was horrified to see it was filled with scores of the hissing, dead-eyed creatures, with hundreds more gathered at the chasm's opposite side. There weren't enough bullets to stop them.

Sophie brought the knife down on the rope that anchored the bridge to the supports. It had been weakened by the century of exposure to the elements but didn't give in as easily as she'd hoped. She sawed at the fibers.

Joseph and Garrett's rifles cracked repeatedly as they picked off the resurrected figures. Sophie kept watch on the advancing army out of the corner of her eye. When a body was felled, it created an obstacle that slowed its companions—but even with the blockades, they were gaining on her position quickly.

The first rope snapped, causing the bridge to lurch dangerously. Three cadavers pitched over the edge and plunged into the thundering river below.

Sophie swiveled and began sawing at the second rope.

Joseph's gun fell silent as he ran out of ammunition, and she heard him swear.

She focused her whole attention on the rope, cutting with all of her remaining strength as the knife's serrated blade split the wet cord, showering dusty fragments of fiber onto the mud below. As she neared the end, the tension finished the job for her, snapping the rope and causing the bridge to career a second time. It held for a second, still tethered by the two ropes attached to the wooden slats, before the increased tension and the cadavers' weight caused them to tear free from their anchors.

The structure fell away. It made a faint whistling noise as it arced through the air, strangely graceful, dropping the corpses into a free fall as they pitched into the gorge and were swept up by the white-froth river.

Sophie collapsed backward, dizzy from mingled stress, fear, and exhilaration. The rope bridge hit the opposite side of the cliffs and was reduced to nothing more than a limp ladder. Above that, corpses continued to mill about the edge of the drop-off and began to hiss and howl their frustration at having no access to their prey.

There was peace for a moment, then Garrett said, "Where's Elise?"

Sophie turned. Joseph leaned against a tree, using it for support to keep his weight off his injured leg. Garrett stepped into the glade and swung around. His expression was frantic. "Where is she?"

Sometime during the fight, Elise had disappeared. A small

part of Sophie hoped she had returned to Kensington, but the far more likely answer was that the Grimlock had resumed control. Bitter frustration tightened her throat as she gained her feet, shaking, drenched, and mud caked.

"Elise!" Garrett yelled then turned and crashed into the forest. "Elise!"

Garrett's footsteps and calls faded as he ran through the trees until all she could hear was a strange blend of the rushing water, the distant corpses' wails, and the spatter of thin, drizzling rain.

"Sophie."

The word was both a request and a command. Joseph, still supported by the tree, held his leg a few inches above the ground. The bandages were drenched in crimson. Sophie felt a swell of panic and stumbled toward him, begging her shaking legs to carry her for a few more paces. "What are you doing here? How did you—"

Anger flashed in Joseph's eye. "What are *you* doing here? What in the world possessed you to leave Kensington?" He dropped the rifle and caught Sophie's wrist, pulling her closer. She cringed at the harsh note in his voice. His fiery black eyes scanned her face, then his grip loosened until he held her hand softly. The anger drained from his expression, and his tone dropped to one of frustration and fatigue. "You promised me you would put your safety first."

Sophie swallowed, trying to keep her voice steady. "The Grimlock had taken Elise into town. I couldn't leave her there."

"Garrett could have gone after her."

She shook her head. "He was already in the forest, searching for a plant." Her attention turned to Joseph's leg, wrapped in sodden, stained bandages, and the cold claws of fear tightened her insides. "How did you get here?"

"I saw you leave." Joseph shifted to lean more of his weight against the tree. "I called after you, but you didn't hear me. So I followed."

"Like this? No—you can't risk any more damage than—"

"Why must you make this so difficult?" Joseph lifted their hands and pressed a kiss to Sophie's fingers. Warmth ran through her, fighting off the chill caused by the rain, and she leaned toward his touch. "What happens to me now doesn't matter. But I *must* keep you safe. I should never have let you come; if I'd known Garrett had no way to leave, I would have set you back on that carriage, locked the door, and had my man drive you home. But I didn't. Instead, we must do whatever we can to keep you whole until the coach returns to take you from this cursed property." His black eyes flashed. "I need you to help me with that. I need you to be safe."

Sophie frowned as she searched her husband's face. His skin was ashen, and dark shadows hung around his eyes. He looked nearly as sick as Elise. "What do you mean, what happens to you doesn't matter? Of course it does—"

He kissed her fingers again, lingering over them lovingly. "No, my dear. I am dying. Forgive me."

Sophie opened her mouth. A dozen thoughts fought to be spoken, but all of them jammed in her throat. *Don't tease me; of course you're not dying. You're one of the strongest men I know. We can heal your leg. You'll be fine. You won't leave me. You* can't *leave me.*

Deep, crushing sadness hung in Joseph's eyes. He seemed to hear her thoughts as clearly as though she'd spoken them. "Come, let's return to the house. Once you're dry and warm, I'll explain. If it's not too much trouble, I would be grateful if you retrieved my gun."

He turned and, using branches and trunks as leverage, began limping through the forest. Sophie watched him go a few paces then snatched up the rifle and pressed herself to Joseph's side. She wrapped his arm around her shoulders. "Lean on me."

He bent closer to kiss the top of her head. Then, together, they began the slow journey back to Kensington.

CHAPTER 22
SECRETS

GARRETT MET THEM AS they emerged from the forest. He looked bone-weary as he took Joseph's other side. "I couldn't find her." He leaned forward to see Sophie around her husband, and his mustache twitched. "Thank you for searching for her."

"Of course." They faced Kensington and began crossing the patchy grass and dead gardens. "How did you know where to find us?"

"Heard gunshots," he grunted.

Once they were inside the house, Joseph sent Sophie to change in the next room. She did so as quickly as she could, struggling out of the wet dress and draping it over the back of a chair before pulling on dry clothes. She wrung excess water out of her hair then braided it as she returned to the parlor.

Miss Bishop's cold gray eyes followed her as she crossed to Joseph. Garrett had already redone the bandages, and Joseph was pulling on a clean shirt.

"Here—let me." Sophie searched her husband's face as she buttoned the shirt. He looked exhausted but smiled at her.

"Garrett has gone to boil some water." He placed his hand over Sophie's when she finished the last button. "You're freezing."

"So are you." She pressed the back of his hand against her cheek. It was alarmingly cool. "But you'll be fine. You just need to rest—" She broke off, and Joseph moved his thumb to caress her skin.

"I didn't want it to be like this," he murmured. The sadness had returned to his voice. "I wished to keep this a secret and let you think my death an accident."

"What are you talking about?" The familiar icy dread was growing in Sophie's chest. Joseph's tone reminded her of how he'd sounded their last day at her father's house, and it terrified her.

Garrett appeared in the doorway, carrying three steaming mugs. Joseph waited for the drinks to be passed about before saying, "Do you remember how the Grimlock injured me during our final day at Northwood, but when I was moved out of the shadow house and back into the real world, the cuts turned to scars?"

"Of course." The white lightning-shaped marks coated his chest. She'd become very familiar with them during their early nights together.

"They're not scars." He inhaled deeply. "At least, they don't behave like regular scars. They're spreading."

Garrett sat on the edge of the coffee table. The wood groaned under his weight, but he didn't heed it. "Explain that."

Joseph kept his attention on Sophie. "You asked your uncle to treat me. At first, we both believed the scars were static, and he even had some hope that they might fade with time. But after a few days, it became apparent that they were spreading—both across the skin and inward."

A ringing filled Sophie's ears. She'd gripped Joseph's hand in both of hers and knew she was holding too tightly but couldn't let go. "H-he can treat it. He's a-a-a good doctor—"

"He's tried, my dear. Everything he could think of. But— possibly because they were created in a supernatural realm and by a supernatural creature—nothing has been able to stop or even slow them." He paused to take a deep breath then continued. "Dr. Hemlock's opinion is that they will continue to spread until they freeze something vital. Either my lungs or my heart."

"No." Sophie shook her head violently then brought Joseph's hand back to her lips so that she could kiss it. "We'll—we'll find some way to fix this—"

"Why didn't you tell us?" Garrett had his arms crossed over his chest, but he leaned forward beseechingly.

"I didn't, at first, because Dr. Hemlock was still trying new treatments. I wanted to wait until I could say there was a cure." Joseph gave Sophie a wry smile. She didn't drop his hand but kept pressing small, frightened kisses to his knuckles. "You had already been through so much—the marriage followed by every- thing that happened at Northwood—"

"You should have told me." The words escaped Sophie as a choked whisper.

"Yes, I should have," Joseph said. "I abhorred the idea of causing you additional pain. But I can't say this route has been any kinder."

Sophie buried her face in his shoulder. He brought his hand up to stroke her hair, brushing the drying strands away from her neck. Garrett heaved a sigh, stood, and crossed to revive the embers in the fireplace.

"How could you think this was kinder?" She'd waited until she thought her voice would be steady, but it still wavered. "I-I would have taken more care of you if I'd known—"

"Which is why I didn't tell you." Joseph's voice was whisper soft as he stroked her hair and neck. "I knew you liked me, but I'd hoped it was still early enough in our marriage to detach your affections."

"Oh." Sophie's eyes opened. "When you didn't come to bed—when you stopped spending time with me—"

"If I'd been a stronger man, I might have attempted to make you hate me." Joseph chuckled. "But I couldn't. I'm too selfish and enjoyed your smiles too much, I'm afraid. The most I could manage was to distance us and hope your affections would wane. That way, my passing might hurt less or even be a relief. You're young and beautiful. If you were to meet a good, kind man—"

They were the same sentiments Sophie's father had expressed the last time they'd talked. She shook her head to cut Joseph off.

He blinked quickly as he tried to rein in his own emotions. "I wish I could stay by your side through your life. But if I cannot do that, I can at least give you the greatest possible chance of happiness by leaving quickly and quietly. When I received Garrett's letter, it seemed like fate. I came to Kensington with no expectations of ever leaving."

Sophie tried to smile, but the expression felt broken and unnatural. "If you were trying to repress my feelings, it was a hopeless cause. I love you."

"I'm so sorry." He met her gaze for a long second then tilted forward and pressed his lips to her cheek. One hand moved to cradle her neck, the fingers featherlight and delightfully precise. "You deserve more than this."

Sophie leaned closer to him, unable to stop herself as she clutched at his shirt and sought his touch. He gave it to her, wrapping his arms about her, his mouth claiming hers.

There was no way to doubt his feelings this time. He cared for her deeply, fiercely, desperately, and every touch expressed it with such exquisite heat that Sophie shuddered when she pulled back. Garrett had been considerate enough to leave the room, but Sophie hadn't even noticed his going.

"How bad is it?" Her fingers drifted to Joseph's chest, to where the scars were hidden under the shirt.

Joseph glanced aside, the warmth in his expression fading. "Your uncle thought it might take weeks—possibly months—before it became deadly. But breathing has been difficult over the last two days."

"Oh." Sophie bent forward. The weight of the discovery was crushing her. *Joseph has already endured so much. He doesn't deserve to die like this. Perhaps I can talk to my uncle—see if there is something they haven't tried yet—surgery or an herb or—*

She rocked back, her eyes wide. "Cessant's bloom!"

"I had the same thought when we found the letter," Joseph said, and Sophie was reminded of how his behavior toward her had shifted after the discovery of the hidden library. "But, my dear, even if we found the seeds, it would take six weeks to grow the plant. I cannot expect to survive that long."

CHAPTER 23
FALLEN STONES

SOPHIE STAYED AWAKE LONG after the men had drifted into fitful sleep. Garrett had offered her the second chaise longue, but she preferred to sit beside Joseph and watch over him. Occasionally he twitched and murmured, but he calmed when she stroked his hair.

Grief coiled through Sophie's insides like a fat, cold snake. It was a familiar feeling; she'd drowned in it following her mother's death. This grief was different, though—a hot rivulet of anger ran through its core, and it burned her.

Joseph had said he was dying, but she couldn't accept it—not while he lay next to her, living and breathing and with his heart beating under her hand. *There must be some way to save him.* The thought ran through her mind a hundred times. *He's not lost yet. There must be something I can do.*

The small clock Garrett had brought with him chimed two

in the morning. Joseph shifted again, his expression tightening from either an uneasy dream or pain, and Sophie murmured soft words as she ran her fingers through his hair.

There must be something I can do. He doesn't think he will live six weeks, but if I could only find the seeds, we would at least have a chance...

Someone exhaled. It was a heavy expression of sadness, the air dragged out of dry lungs, and was wholly different from any sound Garrett could make. Sophie swiveled to face the room.

The clouds had parted and allowed moonlight through the curtains to paint the furniture in an ethereal blue glow. Sophie squinted into the shadows, searching for motion among the decayed chairs and stools and tables. *Has Elise returned?*

The creeping feeling of watchful eyes drew Sophie's attention to the large painting over the fireplace. Miss Bishop's gaze was as piercing and intent as ever, but Sophie thought there might be less pride and less hostility about the countenance. She tilted her head to one side, trying to understand why the portrait gave such a different impression that night, then jolted backward.

The painting had *blinked.*

No, it couldn't have. The poor light is creating illusions.

Sophie kept her gaze centered on the portrait, barely daring to draw breath as she watched the paint.

Except, it wasn't paint. The blended colors had shifted into something very different.

Miss Bishop exhaled, and the dry, rattling breath set Sophie's nerves on edge. She opened her mouth to wake Garrett, but something about Miss Bishop's expression stopped her. The old woman's face had none of the hostility or gleeful cruelty she'd shown when she'd attacked them. Instead, her expression had shifted to something sad and soulful. She leaned forward and stretched one hand out of the painting.

This is a dream, Sophie realized as she watched Miss Bishop carefully climb through the frame and lower herself to the ground. *I must have fallen asleep after all.*

As the woman moved outside of her portrait, her appearance morphed. The healthy skin she'd had in the painting decayed and shriveled. The lips pulled back from her teeth, and her flesh shrank until she seemed nothing more than skin stretched over bones. Most horrifically, the eyes drew into their sockets, withering and sliding back until they disappeared deep into the shadows inside her skull.

I need to wake up. Sophie tightened her hands into fists, digging her nails into her palms, but the dream persisted.

Miss Bishop's boots made a soft clicking noise as they touched the ground. Her dress had darkened and withered to match her body until her appearance corresponded with her form from the first night when Sophie had seen her at the end of the bed.

Don't be afraid. She's not real. You'll wake up in a moment, and everything will be normal.

Miss Bishop inclined her head to Sophie in a silent acknowledgment. More from habit than deliberate choice, Sophie dipped her head in response.

Joseph shifted once again, murmuring something. Sophie felt

behind herself to press her hand to his chest. He was warm and solid, and the steadily beating heart was comforting.

Miss Bishop raised one of the desiccated hands and beckoned to Sophie. She then turned and crossed the room, seeming to glide more than walk, and disappeared through the door.

Sophie remained rooted to the spot. She was shaking, but a heated curiosity had arisen. Unlike the real Miss Bishop, this dream phantom didn't seem at all hostile. Sophie watched the door the spirit had moved through. One minute ticked by, then two, but Miss Bishop didn't return.

It's a dream, Sophie reminded herself as she glanced first at Joseph and then at Garrett. *Nothing bad can happen.*

She went to the door, nudged it open a fraction, and peered through. Miss Bishop stood in the foyer's center, hands folded, as she waited for her companion. As soon as Sophie appeared, she turned and glided toward a door on the opposite side of the room.

She wants to show me something.

Sophie looked at the sleeping men a final time. They were both still and quiet. The mantel's portrait was now empty of subject; the frame and shadowy background were all that remained of the elaborate painting. Sophie turned back to the figure, which had paused in the opposite doorway, then crossed her arms over her torso and hurried across the cracked tiles.

Miss Bishop lingered until Sophie was a dozen paces away, then turned and disappeared into the dark hallway. They moved like that—Miss Bishop pausing any time Sophie lost sight of her—as they passed through the vast manor.

The air, which had been warm in the parlor and cool in the foyer, turned icy as they moved farther from the building's livable spaces. Sophie guessed where they were going a moment before she stumbled into it.

The collapsed wing.

She sucked in a breath as they entered a moonlit room. While her half of it—including the door she'd entered through and the first six feet of walls—was intact, the second half had been reduced to rubble. When she raised her head, she could see a thousand stars competing with the moon to light the area.

In the time they'd spent at Kensington, she'd never entered the collapsed section. It surprised her. When lit by the faint blue glow, the tangle of fallen stones and wooden beams seemed both beautiful and tragic.

Interspersed with the collapsed rocks were pieces of crushed furniture, curtains, carpets, and domestic items. Fragments of a mirror crunched under Sophie's boots when she stepped forward.

Miss Bishop stood farther into the rubble, poised on top of a toppled pillar, waiting for her.

"Where are you leading me?" Sophie called, but the ghost either couldn't or didn't wish to answer.

Sophie sucked in a quick breath, gathered her skirts, and began climbing a collapsed wall. It was a slow, precarious hike. She quickly learned to avoid stepping on shingles, as they slid easily. Every time she drew near Miss Bishop, the dead woman turned and walked farther through the ruins, never taking more than ten steps before turning and waiting again. Unlike Sophie, Miss Bishop walked the path easily.

Sophie soon resorted to using her hands as well as her feet to aid the climb. She tried to count how many rooms they passed through, but it was difficult to tell with little more than the foundations left.

She thought they must be nearing the edge of the building by the time Miss Bishop stopped inside a small hollow and pointed to the ground at her feet.

"What is it?" Sophie crouched to slide off the edge of a horizontal wall.

Miss Bishop didn't answer. Instead, she turned, took one step, and disappeared into nothingness.

Sophie, still clinging to the rocks as her feet sought purchase, gasped. The spirit's departure had been both sudden and fluid. It was almost as though she'd stepped around a corner—except no corner existed.

Sophie gained her feet and approached the space where the ghost had stood. It looked no different from the rubble they'd already traversed. Stones were built up into hills and valleys with aged paraphernalia caught among it like a ship's flotsam half-submerged in a stone ocean.

"What did you want me to see?" Sophie knelt among the rocks and began picking through the debris. A horde of woodlice scuttled out of sight when she lifted a rusted pot. She moved slowly, wary of cutting herself in the poor light, as she peered under an overturned door.

The ornately carved slab of wood blocked the light, but Sophie could just make out a pale oval shape underneath. She squinted and tilted her head to the side as she tried to guess what it was, then she gasped and pressed a hand over her mouth. She was looking at the dome of a human skull.

"Mercy." The dreamlike sensation fled. Sophie blinked and looked around, feeling as though she were seeing her surroundings for the first time. The chilled night air bit at her exposed skin, and little plumes of mist rose from her lips as her breathing quickened. There was no longer any way to delude herself into believing she was asleep.

And that meant...

There's a body in these ruins.

Sophie took a quick lungful of air to steady her shaking hands. She wanted to run back to the warmth and safety of the parlor, but Miss Bishop's spirit had brought her here for a purpose, and Sophie didn't want to leave before she'd completed her task.

Her nerves were taut as bowstrings, but she wedged her feet into a groove in the stone, pressed her fingers to the underside of the door and lifted. The wood groaned under the pressure. Years of rain had eaten at its sturdiness, and as Sophie strained against it, the wood cracked and splintered down its length.

Moving carefully so that she didn't step on the body, Sophie lifted and pushed the broken half of the door over to expose the shape underneath. The wood had protected the body exceptionally well. The flesh was decayed, but the bones were all whole, and even the clothing was largely intact.

"Oh." Sophie moaned as she gazed over the elaborate black-silk dress. "*Oh.*"

Miss Bishop lay on her back, facing the sky, her long, steel-gray hair spread about her skull like a halo. Even in death, she had a regal aura. Sophie stumbled backward until she hit the wall.

We buried the wrong body. She pressed a hand over her thundering heart then turned back to face the way they'd come. The ruins seemed to stretch for miles before the house's silhouette rose to block the stars, but Sophie knew they couldn't be more than fifty paces in length. There was nothing she could do for Miss Bishop that night. She would return to the parlor, wait until morning, then ask Garrett to help her bury the figure. Sophie began climbing the fragment of wall blocking her path then pulled up short as an idea struck her.

A spark of urgent hope flared in the pit of her stomach. She turned, recklessly scrambled back into the hollow where the body lay, and began patting at the dress. A week before, the idea of touching a corpse would have been abhorrent—but Sophie had grown desperate enough that she didn't even flinch when the bones cracked under her hands.

Does she have cessant's bloom? The thought consumed Sophie, pressing her to hunt for pockets and reticules. *Was she carrying it when she died?*

Sophie dipped her hand into where the corpse's bosom had once existed. Her fingers slipped between the hard, grainy ribs and found a leather pouch. She pulled it out as carefully as she could, trying not to damage the skeleton any more than necessary, and tried to control her breathing as she held the bag up to the moonlight.

The leather was old and stained, but cloistered inside the corpse, it had weathered the rain remarkably well. Something heavy and a little larger than Sophie's hand rested inside, and her fingers shook badly as she undid the bag's ties.

A book fell out and landed on the stone with a hard slap. Sophie stared at it, shocked, as disappointment rose up like a wave to consume and extinguish the hope. It was a journal, identical to the ones they'd pored over in the library.

Sophie shook the leather bag, faintly hopeful that she would still find the seeds, but it was empty. She threw it aside and returned to searching the corpse.

She didn't take any chances but hunted through the stiff and tattered skirts, searched both pockets, and even lifted the skeleton's torso a few inches to check underneath. By the time she slumped back against the stone wall, shaking from the cold and with tears stinging her eyes, she was certain Miss Bishop hadn't been carrying the seeds.

Shame forced hot color into her cheeks as she realized the magnitude of her actions. She'd desecrated the corpse and rummaged through it like a grave robber. Miss Bishop's spirit had led her to its resting place, likely in a request for burial, but Sophie had shamed herself and vandalized the body in search for the plant that might save Joseph. Disgrace mingled with disappointment and tightened her throat until it was difficult to breathe.

Sophie would have sat there for longer, but once she'd fallen still, the cold began to eat at her. She shivered, picked up the journal and its bag, tucked both into her skirts, and gave the skeleton one final, regretful look. "Forgive me."

She turned and began climbing through the debris, moving with increased care now that she no longer deluded herself that she was dreaming. She could take risks in her dreams, but reality's consequences for a misplaced step or punctured hand were far more severe.

As she progressed through the ruins, her thoughts returned to the journal. She, Joseph, and Garrett had assumed the book they'd found in Miss Bishop's room—the one containing the letter regarding cessant's bloom—had been her last. But it seemed Miss Bishop had carried her current journal on her person. *At least now we will hear whether she retrieved the seeds.* The thought restored some of Sophie's hope. By the time she reached Kensington's intact rooms, she was eager to rekindle the parlor's fire and read.

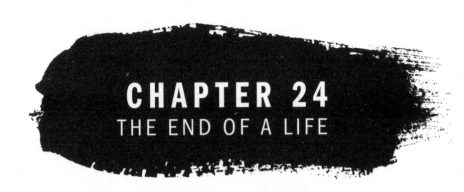

CHAPTER 24
THE END OF A LIFE

IT WAS DIFFICULT TO rouse Joseph, but once he was awake and had heard what Sophie had done, he gave her a glare that would wither plants. "I was under the impression you'd promised not to take risks," he growled.

"I'm sorry." Sophie gave him an apologetic smile. "I truly thought I was dreaming until I found the body."

"What is in the journal?" Garrett, still half-asleep, rubbed at his face. "Does it say anything about the plant?"

Sophie knelt by the fire and fed two fresh logs to the embers. She waited until they'd caught then pulled the book out of her skirts and carefully cracked the cover open. It was a well-made book, and the leather bag, corpse, and wooden door had all worked together to preserve it, but it had not escaped damage completely. Water had soaked the lower corner and made many of the words bleed. The paper felt as though it might crumble under Sophie's touch, and she pried the pages apart with agonizing care. She quickly saw that the journal contained no more than five pages of entries. That unsettled her, and she turned back to the first page to start reading aloud.

"*I received a letter from Edward Danvers today. He has finally agreed to pass his seeds on to me. This is a terrific boon; they will be no direct help against the monster, but I can use their elixir to preserve my own life and that of my brother when the fight comes.*" Sophie raised her head. "So she only wanted the seeds to heal them in case they were hurt."

Joseph nodded. "Of course, during Miss Bishop's time, the Grimlock still lived in the mirror half of the house. It's possible that moving into Elise has made it more susceptible to the plant."

Sophie returned to the book. "This entry is from two days later. *I am soaking the seeds as instructed and will plant them tomorrow. Mr. Trent has grown unwell. There was a storm when he retrieved the seeds from town, and his clothes were soaked through by the time he returned. He has a fever and yet insists on continuing his work. I wish I could command him to rest, but that has never worked in the past.*"

She turned the page. "*Mr. Trent will not wake. He speaks in his sleep, and the fever runs out of control. I do not know what to do. It is two days' ride to summon a doctor; I cannot send Trent, and I cannot go myself for he will die if he is left alone. I can only bathe his face and give him sips of water and pray he overcomes this illness.*"

Sophie had a horrible premonition of where the story was going and almost wished she could avoid turning the page. A cool stillness had fallen over the room; the fire crackled and popped beside her, but otherwise, the house felt too quiet.

"*Mr. Trent deteriorates rapidly. I am frightened. So, so frightened. I beg him to wake, to come back to me, but he no longer talks in his sleep, only breathes too quickly.*"

The next passage was written sloppily, the lines all crooked and the words malformed. Sophie had to read slowly and carefully to make it out. "*John is dead. I buried him in that corner of the forest where we liked to sit on good days. I was not able to dig the grave as deeply as I would have wished, but at least he has rest. I was in a poor mind when I returned from burying him. I saw the seeds had sprouted, and I struck them out of their dirt in a fit of rage.*"

"No!" Garrett barked. He'd shot out of his chair, his face contorted in frustration and grief. "Idiot woman!"

"There's more," Sophie looked back at the page and read the next passage quickly. "*I calmed enough after an hour to return to them. Two were too damaged to save, but I replanted the third sprout. It's small—a thin green stalk and a leaf smaller than my fingernail—but I will tend to it and pray. It is strange; I never felt lonely before, not even on the days when John was away on an errand. But now I feel as though I am the last person on earth. It is hard to go on.*"

Sophie swallowed thickly as she turned the page. Miss Bishop had never been so candid in her other journals; almost all of them had been factual statements of progress or setbacks, interspersed with brief mentions of John Trent. This was the first time Sophie had seen Miss Bishop discuss her own emotions. She could only imagine the agony the older woman must have gone through after losing and having to bury the man she loved.

She scanned the next few pages and relayed their contents. They were all one-line entries detailing the plant's progress. It had survived being torn out of the pot and was growing steadily. The writings were devoid of any other information, though, and Sophie had to wonder how Miss Bishop was coping. If the journal was any indication, her world had shrunk to the little plant growing on her room's desk.

"The first flowers have come in. They are a brilliant sky-blue, and the petals are shaped like small hearts. I see the first seeds already forming in the blooms' centers. I will wait for these flowers to go to seed so that I may plant more."

Sophie turned another page and found herself at the last entry. Unlike the passage that had marked Mr. Trent's passing, this was written far more neatly than the others, almost as though Miss Bishop had taken exceptional care when forming it.

"I received a letter from Northwood. My brother is dead. A section of the roof collapsed on him, crushing him and killing him instantly, they say. There is now no reason to continue in anything. I have thrown the plant away and will await my own death. I pray the next life will be kinder to me than this one has been."

Sophie looked up from the page. Hot tears stung her cheeks, and she wiped them away, but more quickly followed. Joseph, his face grim, held his hand toward her. She went to him and allowed him to pull her to his side and envelop her in his embrace. He kissed her cheeks and her hair but didn't try to speak comfort.

She was grateful for that. There was no relief to be had; Miss Bishop's life had ended in tragedy, and the precious flower was gone. Sophie was no longer surprised that the spirit was vengeful. Even in death, Miss Bishop had no respite.

"That's it, then." Garret had flopped back in his chair, and he stared at the ceiling with dead eyes. "There is no cessant's bloom. You are to die, Joseph, and my daughter will probably follow in a few weeks. I now realize how remiss I was to not bring any alcohol to this cursed hole."

He pushed out of the chair. His gait was unsteady and his face flat as he crossed the room, exited, and slammed the door after himself.

"Don't worry for him," Joseph murmured into Sophie's hair. "He will be angry for three or four hours, but when he returns, he will be calm and practical once again. We cannot give up yet. The bloom is no longer an option for Elise's cure, but that does not mean there is no hope. We simply have to keep looking."

We. It was a sweet word but cut deeply into Sophie's heart. *We* would not exist for much longer. She clung to Joseph, unable to face the idea of letting go and trying not to listen to how labored his breathing had become.

CHAPTER 25
DIRE CHOICES

DAWN ROSE SLOW AND cold. It painted red streaks through the gray clouds and did little to lift the chill from the parlor.

Exhaustion pulled at Sophie, making her limbs feel heavy and her head ache. She hadn't had any rest that night but was reluctant to sleep. Every moment she had with Joseph was precious, and she felt that it would be squandering their time together to doze through it.

Joseph held her enveloped in his embrace, stroking her hair softly. Being so close to him felt good and right, as though her whole life had been in search of that feeling. When he kissed her forehead, rivers of warmth ran through her limbs in spite of the cold room.

At last, as cold rays of sunlight began to reach over the treetops, Joseph lowered her backward. Sophie, half-asleep, mumbled in protest. Joseph only chuckled and kissed her cheek. "You're tired, my dear. Rest for now."

He rose and limped toward the fire. The sleepy fog lifted, and Sophie jolted upright. "Your leg—be careful!"

"It will be fine." His voice was tight, but he smiled easily as he bent to add new logs to the coals. "Resting won't help, so I'll be useful instead."

In the fireplace's flickering light, he looked exceptionally gaunt. Sophie had suspected he'd lost weight as far back as their last breakfast at her father's house, but she hadn't realized how pronounced it had become during their days at Kensington. She crossed to him and wrapped her arms around his torso. He returned the hug and sighed deeply into her hair. "Don't be sad for me, dear Sophie."

Sophie squeezed her eyes closed to stop the tears building there. He was asking the impossible; her heart felt as if it were being slowly shredded, and she was powerless to stop it.

"Garrett," Joseph said, and Sophie raised her head from his chest. "Are you ready to start searching?"

Garrett stood in the parlor's doorway, his face expressionless and eyes bleak. He held a stack of books in his arm and raised them in response to Joseph's question. Sophie recognized them as the books from Miss Bishop's private library. "Back to the start, lad."

Joseph gave Sophie a nudge toward the chaise longue. "Sleep. I'll watch over you."

"No, I want to help." She blinked sleep out of her eyes and held out her hand for a book. "I can be useful."

"Lie down while you read, at least." Joseph's voice was soft and warm in her ear. "Rest your neck."

Sophie nodded, took a book, and curled onto the chaise longue. She was too tired to even realize the strategy behind Joseph's suggestion. Despite focusing on the words as intently as she could, she was asleep within a minute of lying down.

Her dreams were fitful. She saw Miss Bishop crawling out of the painting again and again, looking more decayed and broken each time. She saw Elise standing behind her in a long, dark hallway, laughing delightedly as the lights shone in her eyes. And she saw Joseph—her sweet, beautiful Joseph—lying prone on the floor, his eyes wide and glassy, a trickle of blood running from lips he'd opened but would never again use for speaking.

She jolted awake, breathing heavily, and found Joseph kneeling next to her, concern filling his black eyes. "Are you all right?"

"Fine, thank you." It was a reflexive answer, and she could see Joseph didn't accept it. He stroked hair away from her sweaty face, his brow tight.

"You had a bad dream."

Yes. "Not too bad. It's this house—it makes my sleep uneasy."

"Mine as well. You won't need to endure it for much longer. In two days, the carriage returns, my dear, and my man will take you back to your father's."

There was no *we* or *us* anymore. The overwhelming, crushing grief hit Sophie afresh, and she dropped back down onto the chaise longue.

"Try to sleep a little more." Joseph glanced toward the door. "Garrett and I have finished with Miss Bishop's private library.

We thought we might return to the books in the main library to see if there are any scraps Miss Bishop missed."

It was a weak, sad hope, and they both knew it. But there was nothing more that could be done until the coach returned.

"Have you seen Elise today?" Sophie asked.

"No. Garrett searched for her this morning, but she is hiding again."

Sophie exhaled and looked toward the window. The light, which had been pale at dawn, had turned a dingy gray. Tracks of water ran down the windowpanes. She frowned. "It's raining again."

"It is." Joseph's smile was wry as he watched the window with her. "I think I've had enough storms to last both our lifetimes. I suspect this is at least partly the Grimlock's doing; judging by the gardens and the state of the house, it doesn't normally rain much here."

"You think he's influencing the weather?"

"Yes. I always suspected he had some control over it at Northwood, though he never exercised it much." He turned back to meet Sophie's eyes and gave her a kind smile. "There is some breakfast on the table there. Eat, if you can, and try to rest some more. You've only been asleep a few hours. I'll be in the library with Garrett. It's the room next to this, so we will hear you if you call."

Sophie nodded then tilted up to meet Joseph for a kiss. It was soft and warm and lingering, and she felt him sigh as they broke apart.

"I love you," she whispered.

"And I love you." His fingers touched her cheek as he drew back reluctantly. "Sleep well, my darling."

She watched him leave. He still limped, keeping the weight off his leg as well as he could, but his posture was as straight and strong as ever. Sophie waited until he'd left the room, leaving the door open so that they could hear each other, then pushed herself up.

The hours of sleep had done nothing for her exhaustion, but she was hungry enough to pick at the meal Joseph had left for her. He'd given her cheese, dried fruits, and crackers with butter, plus a cup of water, which she drank eagerly. As she ate, she listened to the murmur of voices coming from the next room over. Joseph and Garrett were forming a plan for where to start in the vast collection of books. She felt a swell of admiration for both of them. Returning to the library had to be soul crushing, but neither of them complained or shirked it.

Sophie set the plate of food aside, half-eaten. She was tired but didn't want to sleep any longer. She considered joining her husband and uncle in the library, but something stopped her. The icy-cold, snakelike grief still coiled through her insides, constricting and crushing all that she was, and an ache of hot anger ran through the sensation. It was as though the snake had plunged its fangs into her and its poison was burning in her veins. *He's not yet dead. Why are you grieving when he can still be saved?*

"How?" Sophie ran her hands through her disheveled hair. "What can I do? How can I help?"

Every door she'd tried to open was locked. Joseph had

already been under the care of the only man she trusted with his treatment—her uncle—and Dr. Hemlock had given it up as a hopeless case. The cessant's bloom had been a brief spark of hope, but more than a century divided her from the miracle plant. Even if there were a doctor or healer who could help, they would be days or weeks away—and Joseph didn't have that long.

But there is one person who might be able to help, the voice inside whispered. *A person who spent her life researching the magical and supernatural.*

Sophie raised her eyes toward the painting above the fireplace. Miss Bishop sat, as always, resplendent in her rich, inky-black dress, her eyes haughty and expression judgmental. Sophie rose and clasped her hands ahead of herself as she stepped nearer to the image.

She's dangerous. She injured Joseph. She tried to kill you.

And yet, she'd also shown a human, empathetic side. She'd stood over her lover's grave. She'd led Sophie to her own body, buried deep in the collapsed half of the building. And the journal entries had hinted at a character far less cruel then the malevolent spirit had been.

What should I make of that? It's as though she has two sides to her personality. Could the Grimlock be affecting her after all?

Sophie licked her lips and took another step forward, closing the distance between herself and the portrait. It was a risk, but she would have taken risks a hundred times more dangerous if they held any hope for the kind, black-eyed man in the room next to hers.

"Miss Bishop?" Sophie's voice came out as a whisper. Her clasped hands shook, and the hairs on her arms stood on end, as though the atmosphere had become electric. "Please, will you help me?"

The painting turned to look at her.

CHAPTER 26
SUPPLICATION AND ANSWER

THE PAINTED WOMAN'S MOVEMENTS were slow, as though breaking out of the two-dimensional bonds was difficult. As the image turned toward Sophie, the paint strokes changed into something quite different just as they had the previous night. The haughty look fell from Miss Bishop's face and was replaced with a gentle, sad smile.

Her hand extended out of the portrait. The light had been too poor to make out any details the night before, but Sophie now saw the spirit was made up of a smokelike substance. The material swirled and coiled, always keeping within a distinct area, as though filling a human-shaped container, then coalesced into something more solid.

As it leaned out of the painting, Miss Bishop's form aged and decayed just as it had the night before. The eyes sank back into the skull, the skin stretched tight and pulled back from the teeth, and the figure withered until it was nothing but skin and bone.

Miss Bishop's extended finger brushed Sophie's cheek. She didn't dare flinch away, afraid that any motion would be taken as rejection and the ghost would vanish, and clenched her hands tightly as she fought the impulse to recoil. The touch was light, but the finger was cold and had an unpleasant texture. *Like touching a corpse.* Sophie swallowed her revulsion.

The hand withdrew, and Miss Bishop slunk out of her painting. Sophie stepped back so that the figure had room to climb to the floor. When Miss Bishop straightened, she had fully transformed into the ghoul that had haunted Sophie's stay in Kensington. Her empty eye sockets fixed on Sophie as she inhaled a slow, rattling breath, her pose proud and tall and powerful.

Sophie struggled to keep her fear out of her voice. "Will you help me? My husband is dying—if there's anything I can do—"

Miss Bishop gave no answer but swept forward, gliding past Sophie and toward the door. This time Sophie didn't hesitate to follow.

A glitter of metal caught her eye as she passed the little side table, and she saw the pistol Garrett had given her the day before. It only had one bullet left, but that was better than being unarmed, and Sophie caught it up and tucked it into her pocket.

They left the parlor and entered the foyer silently. For a moment, Sophie thought the spirit might lead her back to the collapsed portion of the house, but instead, Miss Bishop turned to the front door.

To their left was the door leading to the library. Both Joseph and Garrett were quiet, but Sophie thought she could hear the faint rustle of papers as they pored over the books.

As she followed in the spirit's wake, Sophie marveled at how well Miss Bishop matched her collapsing, cobweb-shrouded building. Both had once been grand, intimidating, and powerful but had fallen to time. Now they still stood tall—regal almost—but without any of the luster or grandeur that they had held in life. They were lonely. Desolate. Forgotten.

Sophie swallowed at the bitter sadness that crept over her. The idea of spending a century alone, as Miss Bishop had, watching her most cherished possessions tarnish and crumble while the world forgot she even existed, sent the ache twisting through her heart again.

Miss Bishop held out one hand as she neared the front door, and the grand wooden slab swung open in silent obedience to her gesture. Outside, the rain was heavy, rebuilding the puddles and tiny rivers that had barely had a chance to dry the day before. Miss Bishop moved into the downpour and took the steps to the front garden.

Sophie hesitated at the door. She glanced behind herself toward the library, where her husband sat. Joseph wouldn't be happy that she was leaving, especially not alone, but her instincts said Miss Bishop did not want company on their journey. It was private—a secret to be held between the two of them—and calling for help would cause Miss Bishop to vanish like a patch of fog caught in the wind.

I cannot afford to lose this chance. Sophie stepped through the door and gasped as the rain, freezing cold and thick enough to drench her in seconds, hit her. *I need to trust Miss Bishop. For Joseph's sake.*

Unlike the night before, the ghost did not stop to check that Sophie was following. She strode across the gardens, navigating the muddy pathways and deceptively deep puddles, without glancing back. Sophie hurried to catch up. It felt wrong to walk abreast of the spirit, so she slowed to match Miss Bishop's pace when she was a half-dozen paces behind.

They left the gardens and began crossing the expanse of grass. Sophie twisted to look behind herself. Kensington was cloaked in gloom, with only two windows lit: the parlor, where she'd slept, and the library, where Joseph and Garrett were. She wondered if either of them would look out the window and see her running through the rain. Her dress's blue color had darkened as it became wet, and she knew the farther she traveled, the more she would blend into shadows and be hidden by the falling rain. Even Miss Bishop, only six paces ahead, was difficult to see in the gloom.

Where is she leading me? They were headed toward the forest. *Does she know of a plant or herb that will help?*

Miss Bishop chose the path leading to the bridge. Sophie followed dutifully, shivering and praying that Miss Bishop didn't intend to lead her to the town. Without the bridge, any help over the gorge might as well not exist.

It was harder to see once the trees' heavy boughs further blocked the light, and Sophie wished she'd thought to bring a lamp. She wanted to take more care stepping over roots and around the hidden holes in the path, but Miss Bishop's pace remained smooth and constant, and Sophie was forced to hurry. All around them, insects, birds, and small animals chattered and screeched at the intrusion. The great trees groaned under the weight of the rain and the steady pressure of the wind, and the drips that hit her were less frequent but larger.

At last, the trees thinned, and she and the specter broke out of the forest and into the small clearing ahead of the gorge. Sophie looked to Miss Bishop, hoping and praying that the bridge that hung limply against the opposite cliff was not a surprise to her guide. Miss Bishop paid it no attention but strode to the edge of the drop-off a few meters to the left of the bridge's remaining supports, stared into the gorge, then turned back to Sophie.

Their gazes met for a second, then the spirit disappeared.

Sophie sucked in a quick breath. It had been so sudden and unexpected that, for a minute, she didn't know what to do. *Has Miss Bishop given up? Is she coming back? Should I return to Kensington?*

The rain continued to fall, drenching her and weighing her down. The insects and animals began to quiet now that Miss Bishop's presence had gone, and even the trees seemed to strain less.

She came here with a purpose, just like last night. She wanted to show me something, surely?

Against both her instincts and better judgment, Sophie crept toward the cliff's edge to the place her companion had looked before vanishing. Her nerves grew tighter with every step until

Sophie was balancing precariously on the very edge of the cliff. She held her breath, leaned forward, and looked down.

The river was just as engorged as it had been the day before, and the noise it made as it roiled into itself was a steady, deep roar that seemed to penetrate Sophie's bones. Very little of the shore remained on either side, and nearly all of the bushes and plants had been torn away. Even some of the rocks had been washed downstream by the water's force.

Lying in the mud at the cliff's base, immediately below Sophie's vantage point, was an unusual shape. Sophie squinted against the water that clouded her vision as she tried to make it out. It was partially dark blue, partially black, and with little bits of fleshy tones—

"Elise!" Her fear of the chasm forgotten, Sophie dropped to her knees and gripped the stone's sharp edge as she peered at the girl. Elise lay facedown, her body twisted at a strange angle and only part of her face visible. She didn't move.

Sophie's mouth dried, and her mind began racing. *How long has she been here? Did the Grimlock drive her to throw herself from the cliffs? Is she still alive?*

She took a deep breath and called, with as much force as she could muster, "*Elise!*"

Her voice was engulfed by the churning water and heavy, drumming rain. Something had heard her, though. Sophie turned to look downstream and felt her heart stutter at the sight of five skeletal figures dragging themselves along the river's edge. *The corpses! The ones that fell when we cut the bridge—they're still down there. They survived the river. And now they're coming for Elise.*

Sophie swiveled to look behind herself, toward the path that led to Kensington. It would take four minutes to run back at full speed. One minute to explain the situation to Garrett. Two minutes to find a rope. Four minutes to return to the chasm. *Too long.*

She pulled the gun out of her pocket. Garrett had heard her gunfire the day before when she'd fought the corpses in the village. She prayed her final bullet would be loud enough to summon him again. She held the gun high above her head, pointed its muzzle toward the sky, and pulled the trigger.

The crack was loud enough to make her flinch. The recoil went through her arm, jarring her, and Sophie threw the now-useless gun aside.

At the base of the gorge, Elise stirred. It was a small motion—a twitch of her hand barely visible through the rain—but Sophie was certain she hadn't imagined it. The girl was alive.

Four minutes for Garrett to reach me. And no way to tell him to bring rope.

Sophie gazed from Elise's form to the corpses. Their bodies had been damaged by the fall and weighed down by mud and rain, reducing their speed as they dragged themselves nearer to the girl, but they were still gaining too quickly for Sophie to wait for help.

I'm not going to watch as they claw at her and eat her. I won't sit by and listen to her screams.

She scanned the cliff leading to Elise. It wasn't perfectly vertical but sloped a little and was pocked with large rocks and small, sickly trees that had dug their roots into the crevices. The climb would be treacherous with rain slicking the handholds, but Sophie had no other options. She stood and clawed her heavy, rain-soaked dress off. The light chemise she'd been wearing under her gown would be easier to move in and less likely to tangle or snag. She then searched the cliff's edge for a handhold, found one, and gripped it with all of her strength.

Please, Garrett, come quickly.

There was no time to wait. Sophie turned and lowered herself into the chasm.

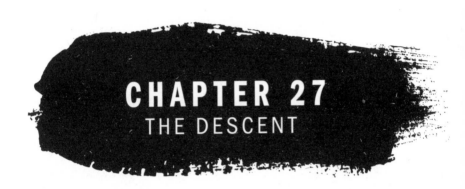

CHAPTER 27
THE DESCENT

SOPHIE'S HEART SET UP a hard, intense tempo as her legs slid over the cliff's edge. She sought purchase in the rocks, found a cranny, trusted it with her weight, then lowered her torso over the edge too.

The wind whipped the thin cotton chemise about her and tangled her wet hair over her face. She moved one leg lower, blindly hunting for a new purchase, and forced herself to release her grip on the top of the cliff once she'd found it.

A strange recklessness had overtaken her. It drowned out the fear that had once ruled her whenever she drew near the chasm, and it pushed her to move more quickly and trust her footholds more readily than she otherwise would have. A thousand thoughts crowded her mind—Joseph's illness, Garrett's frustration, Miss Bishop's unpredictable and deadly temperament. They were all tied to the one cause—the same one that had undoubtedly resulted in Elise's fall. *The Grimlock.*

Anger joined the recklessness, and Sophie increased her pace yet again. She didn't watch the gorge's base draw nearer but only glanced down to hunt for a new boulder, hole, or tree that might support her weight. Several times, she found no such help and was forced to scuttle sideways or even climb a foot or two higher in order to correct her path. The freezing rain numbed her fingers and blurred her vision, the rocks were slippery under her hands, and the bushes were as much obstacles as support, but she pressed on, steadily dropping lower.

Joseph expects me to go home. He thinks I will be able to return to a quiet life with my father and spend my days visiting friends, entertaining guests, going to parties...

She trusted the wrong rock, and it gave way under her boot. Sophie shrieked and scrabbled at the wall, grasping for purchase, and she found it. She clung to the cliff face and sucked in quick, deep breaths. Her fingers, knees, and cheek ached from where they'd been scraped, but she didn't permit herself more than a dozen seconds before she began climbing again.

He's wrong. The Grimlock has abused the most precious people in my life. I'll see it destroyed—even if it takes every remaining moment of my life.

The gorge's floor was growing near, but so were the resurrected townspeople. Sophie could hear their dry, rattling breaths as they struggled through the mud. She glanced below herself and tried to gauge the distance. She was nearly at the ground—no more than six feet, she thought—but the corpses were close to Elise. There was no time to climb the remainder of the distance;

she closed her eyes, said a second's prayer, and leaped off the rock wall.

The chasm's floor had turned to mud. Even so, the landing jarred Sophie badly, and she rolled to her side, gasping and choking against the grit and rain that flooded her mouth. She crawled to her hands and knees and wiped the sludge out of her eyes.

She'd landed a few feet away from Elise and desperately wanted to check on the girl, but the corpses were nearly upon them. Sophie cast around for a weapon. The rocks near the base of the gorge were more crumbled than near the top, and she grabbed one that jutted out of the cliff, ignoring how badly her fingers ached from the cuts and the cold. The rock came free, and Sophie twisted, aimed at the nearest corpse, and threw it.

Her energy had been sapped by the climb. Although the rock hit its mark and threw the skeletal figure backward, it wasn't enough to stop it from snarling as it rose out of the mud.

Sophie grabbed a smaller rock—one the size of her fist—and threw it with all of the strength she had left. The smaller projectile was more effective; it smashed through the skull, and the figure crumpled.

Its two companions were drawing close, and Sophie was forced to scramble out of their reach. She retreated as far as Elise and pulled a fresh rock from the cliff side. This time her aim was shaky, and the rock glanced off the corpse's shoulder. She seized another stone, threw it, and was rewarded with a crunching noise as the skull was dented. But unlike the first corpse, this one didn't fall.

There was no more time; the figures were within reaching

distance, and Sophie couldn't retreat any farther without leaving Elise vulnerable. A sickly, half-dead tree poked out from the cliff, and Sophie fixed on one of the lower branches. It was brittle and snapped off when she applied her weight to it. Sophie staggered to her feet, breathing hard, and swung her branch at the nearest skeletal figure.

The makeshift bat knocked it backward but didn't kill it. Sophie followed quickly, swinging her weapon again, raining blows on the cadaver until dizziness and exhaustion threatened to topple her. The corpse lay in a crumbled mess. Its jaw worked, and rattling breaths escaped a tear in its throat, but she'd broken it enough that it wouldn't rise again.

She turned to face the final attacker, but it had gained on her while her attention had been diverted, and its bony fingers fixed around her ankle before she could leap out of the way.

The corpse used its grip on her to pull itself forward, and Sophie's foot slipped in the mud. She cried out and fell, landing heavily and winded by the impact. The branch skidded out of her reach. The reanimated body didn't waste the opportunity but began to crawl closer, its fingers digging into her skin cruelly, its jaw flexing as it sought her throat.

Sophie swung her fist at it, praying that she would have enough strength to knock her attacker off. She snapped its head back but failed to break through the bone. It snarled, its decayed face contorting in fury, and its teeth grabbed her forearm.

She cried out and kicked at it, struggling to break free and reach her branch, but the cadaver's grip was too tight. She rolled instead, hoping the motion might shake her attacker and release her from the sharp, cutting pressure of its teeth.

They hit a hard object, and Sophie opened her rain-blinded eyes long enough to see they'd tumbled close to the river's edge. They'd bumped against a boulder, and just a foot away, the water churned into an angry white froth.

Please let this be enough.

She rolled over again, carrying the clinging, gnawing body with her, and screamed as they both plunged into the water.

The cold cut nearly as badly as the teeth in her arm. She'd underestimated the power of the water, and she reached for the boulder a second too late. The current snatched her away as her fingers grazed its edge, and then she was forced under the water, tumbled, thrown, and smashed into a rock. The grip on her arm disappeared, but Sophie barely noticed. Her mind was a frenzy of panic, screaming at her to grab onto anything, to get her head above water, to not open her mouth until she could inhale air.

The current had forced her against another boulder, and Sophie scrambled at it, fighting not to lose her purchase, and climbed it until her head broke above the froth and she could suck in a hungry gasp. Her heart felt as though it were about to burst, and every muscle ached from the beating she'd taken. She shook her head and blinked frantically to clear the water from her eyes, and she could have cried from relief when she saw that her rock connected to shore.

Moving slowly, cautious against being snatched back into the pounding, crushing current, Sophie edged to the riverside until she could grip the muddy ground and stagger to her feet.

She stood on the shore for a moment, breathing deeply and trying not to collapse. Her arm ached. She spared it a glance and saw blood welling in the teeth marks, but at least it wasn't bleeding freely. Her legs were shaking and threatened to drop her back to the ground, but they weren't broken. Most importantly, the final cadaver had disappeared into the torrent, where the water would drag it kilometers away before it could escape.

That left Elise. For a second, Sophie panicked that she might have landed on the wrong shore, but a glance at the opposite cliff reassured her. The rope bridge was still visible against the rocks.

She turned and staggered upriver, trying not to pay attention to the stabbing pain that traveled up her jarred leg and the stinging cuts in her arm. Elise came into view after a few minutes, and Sophie increased her stumbles into a quick limp. The girl looked unnaturally peaceful. Her wet black hair was thrown carelessly behind her, and one arm was extended as if in supplication. She'd landed in one of the few areas that still contained plants, and small flowers grew around her skirts.

Please don't let me be too late.

Sophie dropped to her knees at Elise's side and brushed the hair away from her face. The girl's eyes were half-open, and they fluttered at Sophie's touch.

"Elise?" Sophie bent closer, horrified at how cold the child's skin felt. "Can you hear me, sweetheart?"

"*Hh—hhh—*" Elise's lips moved but wouldn't form words.

The fingers on the nearest hand twitched, but that was the only sign of life.

Her spine is broken. The realization made Sophie double over, clutching at her stomach as she fought against the furious, grief-filled scream that built inside her. *No, it can't end like this.*

A loud thud made Sophie jump. She swiveled, preparing to fight any attackers who had crept up behind them, and saw a door lying in the mud.

It was such a surreal, unexpected sight that for a second she thought she might be dreaming. That was impossible, though; the cuts and bruises hurt too much to be imagined.

Sophie raised her eyes and saw that each end of the door had been connected to a rope. The ropes snaked up the side of the cliff, and at the top stood two silhouettes peering down at them.

Joseph. Garrett. They heard the gun. Sophie tried to call to them, but she was still breathless, and her words were swallowed by the river's roar.

The taller, thinner figure gestured, and Sophie looked back at the door. A piece of paper had been forced under where the rope strained tight against the wood. She scrambled forward and pulled it free with shaking hands.

It was written in a hurried but neat script. *If not hurt, place Elise on door and climb up beside. If hurt, wave and wait for assistance.*

Sophie assessed herself quickly. She was hurt, yes, but nothing that would prevent her from climbing. She gazed up the length of the cliff. She'd become tired from climbing down; how much worse would the ascent be? But it was the fastest way to get both herself and Elise to safety, so Sophie took a deep breath and turned to move the girl.

Elise was a deadweight. Sophie pulled her onto the door as gently as she could, trying not to twist the spine any more than was necessary. The girl gave a faint, high whine as she was rolled over but was otherwise quiet.

Sophie centered her charge on the board, gave it a quick check to make sure it wasn't likely to overbalance, then tugged on one of the ropes to signal they were ready. The ropes went taut, then the door rose out of the mud with a thick sucking noise. Sophie sought and found purchase in the rocks and pulled herself up alongside the board. Her muscles protested, but she managed to gain the first few feet quickly. She stayed abreast of the door and watched for any sign that it was about to tip, but the men had tied the ropes in such a way that it stayed even except when it snagged on rock outcroppings or plants. In these cases, Sophie had to wedge herself against the stones as well as she could and push the board around the obstacles.

It was slow, exhausting work and took far longer than Sophie had thought she could stand. She had been climbing for close to half an hour by the time her limbs shook too badly to find any new grip. They were nearing the top of the cliff, but Sophie couldn't move any farther. She slipped back down into a nook that fortunately held her weight, and she tried to focus through the sparks that danced in her vision.

Someone called to her, but she couldn't make out the words. The board began moving again, rising higher and soon vanishing over the edge of the cliff. A few minutes later, a scraping noise alerted her to someone descending nearby.

"C'mon, girl," Garrett's gruff voice said, and his thick arms pried her away from the crevice she'd found. "Up we go."

CHAPTER 28
TEA

SOPHIE'S EYES ACHED WHEN she tried to open them. She could sense the light was muted, but it still felt too bright. Voices spoke nearby, whispering, and she strained to make out the words. "...no horse even. Traveling by foot will take too long—"

She tried to sit up, and the voices fell quiet. A hand appeared behind her head and raised her, then a cup touched her lips. "Drink," Joseph instructed.

Sophie did as she was told. As she swallowed the first mouthful, she realized how thirsty she was and grabbed the cup to drink more deeply. It was only water, but it was one of the best things she'd ever tasted.

"Easy," Joseph said, holding the cup steady. Sophie finished it and took a deep breath. All of the aches and pains were starting to return, but so was an awareness of where she was.

They were back in the parlor. The fire had been built into an inferno, and the room would have been bordering on uncomfortably warm if she hadn't still been wearing the soaked cotton chemise. She'd been wrapped in blankets, though, and laid on the second chaise longue. Sophie twisted to catch a glimpse of the chair opposite Miss Bishop's portrait and saw Elise lying on it, her eyes closed. Garret knelt beside his daughter, his face murderous.

She licked her lips and tried to speak. "Is she—"

"She's alive." Joseph's tone was soft and infinitely sad as he started to ease Sophie back onto her bed. "But severely hurt. Garrett and I were discussing whether to go for help."

Sophie ignored Joseph's gentle pressure and pushed herself back into a sitting position. "But the nearest town is days away by coach—"

"Yes. Without a horse, the journey would be slower than waiting for my man to return." Joseph glanced toward his uncle then leaned closer to Sophie and lowered his voice until she had to strain to hear it over the fire's crackles. "He is near impossible to reason with. I'm afraid there is not much we can do for Elise except make her comfortable; she has been coughing blood. I do not expect her to survive the night."

Sophie struggled to breathe around the rising anger and grief. Something niggled at the back of her mind, something important, but she was still disoriented, and the memory danced away before she could catch it.

"My dear." Joseph caught her in his shockingly intense gaze. "What you did was very foolish. Brave, but foolish. It's a miracle you're not hurt more severely."

There was no anger in his expression, but she caught a glimpse of smoldering panic in the back of his eyes. She'd frightened him, she realized. She pressed her palm to his cheek, wanting to stroke the expression away, and Joseph's eyes fluttered closed as he leaned into her touch.

"I love you too much to lose you." His words were a featherlight breath on her palm. "I thought my heart might stop when I heard the gun and found you were missing. And then to see you at the base of that cliff…" He kissed her palm, inhaled deeply, then rose and placed the cup back on the table. "Are you in much pain?"

"No. No, I'm fine." Sophie looked at her arm and saw someone had bandaged it while she was asleep. The fiery sting had dulled to an ache.

"Would you like to come into the next room so I can help you change? I'd prefer to get you into something dry before you catch cold on top of everything else." Joseph reached out to help Sophie to her feet, but then Elise coughed. Sophie startled at the sound, and the memory—the one that had evaded her while her awareness was still returning—struck her and she grasped Joseph's hand with a small cry.

"Has Elise woken at all?"

Joseph glanced toward the child, and his expression darkened. "Once. Briefly."

"Did she have the Grimlock's lights in her eyes?" Sophie thought back to when she'd knelt by Elise on the chasm's floor. Elise's eyes had been half-closed, but Sophie didn't think they'd held the Grimlock's presence.

Joseph looked confused. "No. She seems to be herself for now."

"Then the Grimlock might have left her." Sophie spoke quickly, her mind racing. "It might have thought the fall would kill her and left of its own free will."

"What does it matter?"

They both turned toward Garrett, who had spoken. His voice was thick with unshed tears and bitterness. "She will live her last day without the monster—a great blessing indeed."

"No—no—" Sophie choked on the words as she tried to explain. "We have to be certain the Grimlock has gone—"

She hadn't released her grip on Joseph's arm. His eyes darted over her face, and his brow lowered. "What's wrong, my dear? What is it?"

Instead of answering, Sophie reached into her cotton chemise's bustier and pulled out a small, slightly crushed plant. She held it toward Joseph, silently imploring him to understand.

He stared at the flower for a second then drew a sharp gasp. "Cessant's bloom."

"What?" Garrett turned abruptly, and his gaze fixed on the thin, delicate plant.

It was small and spindly, barely larger than Sophie's hand, and a dozen tiny blue flowers with heart-shaped petals sprouted from the ends of its shoots. "It was in the gorge. I saw them on the day we arrived here—I remember looking over the side of the bridge and seeing that the ground was covered in blue flowers—but the storm has washed almost all of them away. Elise landed in a patch of the only remaining plants."

Garrett rose slowly. He didn't blink or shift his gaze as he stepped closer. "But how—"

"In the journal, Miss Bishop said she threw the plant away," Sophie said. "Her partner had died just weeks before, and she'd just heard news of her brother's demise. She was grief-stricken and furious, so she tossed the plant away in spite. And is there anywhere that would feel more final or more cathartic than casting the flowers into the chasm?"

Excitement lit up Joseph's face. He cupped Sophie's hand in his, staring at the flowers with dawning realization. "And on that final day, the plant was very near seeding. And the riverbed would have been damp enough for the seeds to soak—"

"And sprout more plants," Sophie agreed, nodding quickly. "So they've continued through the last hundred years, multiplying—"

"And you found them." Joseph clasped her shoulders and kissed her. It was sudden, fervent, and so unexpected that Sophie laughed when they broke apart. "Brilliant woman." He ducked in for a second brief kiss. "Untamable, frustrating, delightful creature."

Sophie felt color rush through her face and quickly adjusted the blanket around her shoulders so that it wouldn't slip too low. "I wasn't even looking for them; they were just growing next to Elise, and I thought it was strange how the petals were blue and heart-shaped just like in Miss Bishop's description. It was more impulse than anything else that made me pick one."

A strange, huffing sound startled Sophie. She turned to see that Garrett's face had turned red. Fat tears ran down his cheeks, and he rubbed at them with gruff embarrassment. "She's saved," he mumbled. "My child is saved."

Sophie's smile faded. She glanced back at the plant and swallowed. The next piece of information was excruciatingly difficult, and she phrased it carefully. "Perhaps. But we have to be sure the Grimlock has gone."

"What?" Garrett took another step forward. "No, we need to make the tea before her condition deteriorates too far."

Sophie licked at her lips and glanced at Joseph for support. His own excitement was fading as he saw the caution in her face. "What is it, my dear?"

"The Grimlock has wanted cessant's bloom too. Do you remember when we discovered E.D.'s letter? The very next day, the Grimlock led Elise to town to search for the seeds. When I found her, she said the Grimlock had been furious—it was angry that the seeds had been taken." She didn't dare meet either man's gaze as she continued in a rush. "And…and I believe the Grimlock made Elise climb down the cliff to retrieve the flowers. I suspect she'd been listening outside the parlor when we read the diary last night, and the Grimlock made the connection with the plants in the riverbed. It sent her there to pick them, but she slipped on a wet rock and fell, and…" Sophie trailed off and glanced at Elise. The girl's breathing was thin and pained.

"Why would the Grimlock want cessant's bloom?" Joseph's dark eyes danced over the plant as he thought.

"I don't know. But I feel it's important to keep the flowers from him."

"He might have wanted to destroy them," Garrett said. "He might have known they were the only way we could save Elise, and he thought to rid us of them before we even found them."

"That's possible." Joseph sat on the edge of the chair and rubbed his hand over his mouth. "But Sophie's concerns are valid. The Grimlock may want the plant for its own benefit."

"It should be safe as long as the Grimlock is no longer inhabiting her," Sophie said. "I couldn't see the lights in her eyes when I found her in the chasm, and Joseph said she seemed to be herself when she woke. It may be that the Grimlock believed his charge dead and abandoned her."

"Where would it go, though?" Joseph asked. "My understanding is that it was only able to latch onto Elise because it had forged a strong bond with her during the months predating Northwood's burning—and even then, it had needed to feed on Rose to have enough energy to make the jump. If it left Elise, it would have no replacement and no haven to tie it to the mortal realm."

Sophie didn't have an answer for that. She dared to glance at Garrett, and the pain in his expression crushed her.

"Please," he rasped. "She's dying. We have to try."

"From what I see, there are two questions we have no way of answering." Joseph frowned at the patchy carpet as he thought. "First, is the Grimlock still possessing Elise? And second, what purpose does it have for cessant's bloom? It must have wanted the plant badly to try to climb down the cliff."

Elise shifted on the chaise, and her face scrunched up from

pain. She was little more than skin and bones, and her skin was ashen. A sinking sensation filled Sophie. *Joseph is right. She won't survive the night.*

"We can deal with consequences after," Garrett said. "This is the only way to save my daughter; we'd be fools not to take it!"

Joseph sighed and ran his fingers through his hair. When he answered Garrett, he did so quietly and with a great deal of care. "We were prepared to die to end the Grimlock's reign."

"*We* were! My daughter was never part of that agreement," Garrett snarled. He seized Joseph's jacket and seemed prepared to shake him, and Joseph placed a hand on his uncle's arm.

"Be rational." Joseph's voice was low. "I do not want to see Elise suffer any more than you do. But what if the plant returns the Grimlock to control over her or gives it increased power? Would you wish your daughter to spend the rest of her life ruled by that monster?"

The anger bled out of Garrett's face. He released his grip on Joseph and stepped back, and when he spoke, his voice cracked. "Of course not."

Joseph looked toward the fire, his expression dark with worry. "If we had more time, we might wait for Elise to wake and monitor her for a few days to be sure. But we don't have that luxury tonight." He turned to Sophie, and the dancing firelight accentuated the shadows about his eyes and the hollows in his cheeks. "Your intuition has not failed you yet, my dear. What do you think?"

Sophie looked back at the plant clasped in her hand. It was

small and innocuous looking. "We don't even know if it will work," she murmured. "We hunted for it based on a rumor a botanist included in his book. For all we know, this could be a common weed with no more healing ability than grass." She glanced back at Elise. "But I would rather try and fail than not try at all."

Joseph smiled. "Yes. I think this is a risk we must take. I'll fetch the water."

"No, stay. I'll be faster." Garrett was already halfway across the room as he spoke. His motions were all quick and sharp, and Sophie could sense he was barely containing his energy. As Garrett left the room, Joseph shifted to sit next to Sophie. She laced her fingers through his, and he lifted their entwined hands to kiss her knuckles. She leaned against him as they waited.

The dizziness from her climb had subsided, but the weariness was grinding her down. Despite their precarious situation, Sophie wanted nothing more than to close her eyes and drift into sleep in her husband's embrace. "Miss Bishop led me to the plant," she mumbled as Joseph stroked her hair. "I don't think she's evil. The Grimlock must have been influencing her."

"You may be right." Joseph kissed her forehead. "I suspect it's been draining Elise's strength, which is why she has been so unwell. That must be how it had the energy to resurrect the townspeople."

"It gains its power through humans?"

"Yes. That's why the deaths at Northwood were all violent and occurred while the victims were still healthy. When the bodies were passed through the red door, the Grimlock would then feed on their energy and gain control over their forms. Without Elise's strength, it would be virtually powerless; it last fed on Aunt Rose, and I suspect it used all of that energy to transfer its anchor from the house to my cousin."

Quick footsteps told them Garrett was returning, and Sophie reluctantly left the warmth and comfort of Joseph's embrace. Garrett was breathless as he entered the room, and urgency was painted over his face. "Make the tea. Quick."

He held out a small pot half-full of water, which Sophie took. The instructions for making the tea were in the water-stained letter, which Garrett and Joseph had left with the botany book on the side table earlier that day. Joseph read while Garrett paced. "Collect the flowers, boil in a small pot of water, and administer to the unwell person."

Sophie swallowed. "It's not very clear, is it? How many flowers and how much water?"

"We'll have to guess." Joseph looked toward the pot. "Tip some of the water out, I think. There shouldn't be any more than one person can swallow easily. We'll add all of the flowers to be sure."

Sophie carried the pot to her empty cup and prepared to tip out some of the excess, but hesitated. "You should have some, too—"

"Not tonight." Joseph's voice was soft and kind. "We don't know how much of the brew is needed to cure someone. My situation is not dire, and we can collect a second plant tomorrow; I would rather have Elise drink it all than take risks by dividing it and making it impotent."

Sophie nodded reluctantly. Her hands shook as she poured out the water until only a large mouthful remained. She then set the pot down and began picking the flowers off the plant.

Elise made a small sound of distress, and Garrett crossed to her. He murmured reassuring words as he wiped her hair away from her sweaty face. "Hold on just a little longer, my dear. Not long now."

Sophie second-guessed her every action as she prepared the tea. Was she supposed to add whole flowers or just the petals? How long did it need to be boiled? She followed Joseph's lead and took no chances; the entire flower was added, and she even used those that had begun to wilt and go to seed. Then she wrapped the end of her blanket around the pot's handle and set it on the fire.

The blaze, built to warm the drenched parties, had been made larger than normal, and the blistering heat forced Sophie to step back after a moment. She took her place beside Joseph, and the three of them watched the blue flowers swirl in the roiling water.

The room felt dangerously still. Elise's breathing was faint enough to be drowned by the fire's crackles and pops and the steady drum of the rain on the windows. The dancing firelight, their only illumination, made shadows snake over the walls and coagulate about the portrait. Miss Bishop watched over them with her familiar disdainful, piercing glare. *Please,* Sophie begged silently, *let these flowers work.*

As the water boiled, the blue color began to leech out of the petals and infuse the liquid. Sophie left it on the flame for nearly five minutes until the flowers were pulpy and pure white and the water had become an odd, thick teal color. She then used the blanket to lift it off the heat and set it on the small table. "It will need to cool."

"Can you fan it?" Garrett still hovered over his daughter. "She's growing worse."

Sophie tucked the blanket around herself then used the botany book to swirl cool air over the steaming liquid. Joseph rose, limped to the sideboard, and retrieved a second cup. As soon as the steam subsided and the liquid looked cool enough that it wouldn't scald, they poured it into the beaker.

It had thickened into a syrup, and the teal had become a deep, stormy turquoise. She passed it to Garrett, who knelt beside his daughter and pressed the cup to her lips. "Drink," he urged. "Please."

She didn't stir. Garrett's breath was quick and anxious as he lifted the girl's head and tipped the liquid into her mouth.

"Be careful, or she'll choke." Joseph took Sophie's hand, and she could feel his fingers trembling.

The water had boiled down to only a few tablespoons, and Garrett poured it all into Elise's mouth. He then rubbed at her cheek until she swallowed, and laid her back down. "Come on, my dear," he growled, setting the cup to the ground. "Wake up."

The storm outside seemed to redouble. Sophie tightened her grip on Joseph's hand and pressed herself to his side. His attention was focused on Elise, his lips tightened into a thin line and his brow constricted.

Then doors began to slam, one after another, starting at the far side of the house and drawing closer, their bangs becoming increasingly loud. Thunder crashed overhead, drowning out Sophie's frightened gasp, and a gust of wind rushed through the room, chilling her and sending papers fluttering around them like snowflakes. Sophie caught glimpses of the papers as they rushed past her, brushing her cheek and catching at her hair. They were Elise's drawings. The black, misshapen creature loomed out of each page, its lamp-like eyes staring at her from a hundred directions.

Then a rush of wind surged down the chimney, wiping out the fire in an angry sizzle. The three candles that had been spaced about the room flickered and died a second later, and cold, hard terror constricted Sophie's chest.

The room was pitch-black. She could feel Joseph's hand squeezing hers and hear the rustle of his clothes as he twisted to peer through the blackness, but she couldn't see a thing. The darkness seemed unnaturally heavy, as though there were an ocean of it engulfing them, miles deep, and with no hope of swimming out.

A deep, rattling inhalation broke the stillness. It was a sound that had haunted Sophie's nightmares for weeks, and she shrank away from it reflexively. Then two huge, lamp-like eyes opened, shining like candles in the darkness, as the Grimlock awoke.

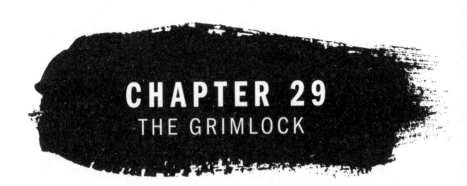

CHAPTER 29
THE GRIMLOCK

THE FIRE BEHIND THEM fizzled and hissed then flickered back to life. Its glow extended through the room slowly, bringing first the chairs, the small tables, and the stacks of books into relief before finally lighting the two massive, clawed feet, the bowed legs, the thick body, and the cruel, twisted countenance of the Grimlock.

It was naked, bestial, and entirely black, and its smooth, glistening skin stretched over taut muscles. When it smiled, its sharklike teeth glittered in the dim light, and its eyes—not really eyes, but hollows with white lights inside—glowed more vividly.

"Thank you." Its voice sounded like metal scraping across gravel to Sophie's ears. "You've saved me a great deal of inconvenience."

Sophie didn't dare move as her mind raced to comprehend their new situation. Elise still lay on the chaise longue, neither moving nor breathing, and Garrett was collapsed on the floor next to her, a trickle of blood running down his temple. The

Grimlock stood before them in the flesh, so tall that its head nearly scraped the ceiling. The only other time Sophie had seen it had been in Northwood, when it had lived inside the mirror house hidden behind the red door. Now it stood whole and solid in the physical realm.

An herb to make what is broken whole. The passage from the botany book came back to Sophie, and she felt sick as she realized what they'd done. They'd searched for the plant with the intent of healing Elise, but the Grimlock itself, being nothing but a presence inhabiting a body that did not belong to it, was itself *broken*. Instead of healing Elise, the plant had healed the beast afflicting her.

The Grimlock stretched its limbs, and the long claws clicked against each other as it flexed into an animalistic crouch. "Get the door, my pretty. It would be such a shame if any of our guests left before dinner was finished."

For a moment, Sophie couldn't think whom the Grimlock was speaking to, then she turned sharply as the door's lock clicked. The veiled woman stood with her back to the wood, her head bowed toward the Grimlock as though in deference and her face hidden by the veil.

Miss Bishop. So the Grimlock is controlling her after all.

Then the woman tilted her head, almost as though she were listening to a noise Sophie couldn't hear, and the dark veil slipped to the side to expose a slice of her face. She was grinning insanely, and a single black eye, barely visible in the dim light, watched them with insatiable hunger.

A wave of horror hit Sophie. *That isn't Miss Bishop. This woman's eyes are black; Miss Bishop has no eyes, and even during life, her irises were gray. They both wear black dresses, but they are not the same—how did I not see it before?*

Joseph sucked in a sharp breath, and he said a name that sent chills through Sophie. "Rose."

The veiled woman's teeth parted as she exhaled a sharp "*Ha!*" noise.

She should be dead! Sophie's mind protested, frantic in its fear. *I saw the Grimlock eat her! But—of course—she is dead. The Grimlock brought her back.*

Suddenly, the veiled woman's actions made sense. Miss Bishop had stood at the end of Sophie's bed on her first night at Kensington, watching over the new intrusion into her home. She had also stood by her lover's grave, led Sophie to her skeleton, and guided her to Elise and cessant's bloom. It was Rose, though, who had appeared in the mirror, attempted to choke Sophie, and damaged the chandelier's anchor.

Rose's long, bony hands twitched at her sides. Except for her black eyes, she was nearly unrecognizable as the stiff, cultured woman who had tormented Sophie during her stay at Northwood. She seemed to still hold a human awareness in a way that the village's reanimated corpses did not, but death had made her truly insane.

The Grimlock shifted its weight, bending forward slightly, and both Joseph and Sophie took a half step back.

"This is so delightful, my pretties." Its words sounded so harsh and guttural that Sophie wanted to clasp her hands over her ears to block the sound out. "We are all gathered together—a reunion, of sorts. I was afraid I might have to hunt you down, dear Joseph, and you, sweet Sophie, but you saved me the effort by coming to visit. As I said, you've been remarkably considerate."

Joseph moved forward so that he stood between Sophie and the two creatures. Sweat shone on his forehead as his hands tightened into fists. "Use a chair," he hissed, his voice so low that Sophie could barely hear it. "Break the window. *Run.*"

She glanced behind them. The large window's frame was badly decayed, and many of its panes were already fractured, allowing droplets of rain to pass through. Outside was pitch-black, and the storm was so tumultuous that Sophie doubted they would even be able to run in a straight line. Fleeing would be useless even if Joseph came with her. And leaving without him was not a possibility she would consider. That left them with one option: fighting. She glanced across the room to where Garrett's knife sat on the little side table. It was the only weapon she could see, and she would have to pass the monster to reach it.

"I would stay and chat a little longer, but I find myself desperately hungry. Elise was not quite as nourishing as I would have wished." The Grimlock's voice held clear amusement. "I hope you'll forgive me if I save any closer acquaintance until after I've fed."

He lunged toward them. The motion was so quick and fluid that Sophie had no time to react. She felt the impact and fell backward, but the claws did not cut her. Instead, Joseph hissed as he was slammed into the floor. He'd caught up one of the chairs and was using it as a barricade between him and the beast.

The wind increased, rushing down the chimney, kicking up the scattered drawings and threatening to douse the fire a second time. Sophie scrambled toward the knife at the other side of the room. The Grimlock and Joseph crashed past her, forcing her to duck to avoid being snared in their fight. It was not a fair contest; Joseph had managed to wedge the chair between himself and the Grimlock, but the beast's teeth were crushing the fragile wood, and the lights in the monster's eyes flared brightly as it struggled to bring its jaws closer to Joseph's neck.

I have to stop it. I have to keep him safe, somehow—

She caught the edge of the table and reached for the knife, but a gnarled, decaying hand slammed over it before she could touch the metal. Rose loomed above her, lips stretched wide in a viciously happy grin.

There was no time to react; the back of Rose's hand smacked Sophie's cheek so hard that her vision flashed to white. The blow knocked her down; she rolled over to avoid a second attack as hot, metallic blood coated her tongue.

She opened her eyes to see Joseph fall to the floor. The chair had been torn away, and he gasped, contorted, and coughed blood onto the carpet. She tried to crawl toward him. His shirt and hair were soaked in red, with more blood welling in the wounds even as she reached toward him.

The great black beast loped forward and pressed its foot onto Joseph's chest, pinning him to the floor and causing him to choke from the pain. The Grimlock bent its spine until its maw was inches above Joseph's face. "Such a foolish child," it purred. "Had you been willing, you might have joined your aunt as one of my servants. Eternal life at my side. Would that really have been so bad?"

Hatred twisted Joseph's face. Instead of answering, he brought his hand up, smashing the palm into the space between the Grimlock's eyes. The beast threw its head back, howling, as drops of black blood spat out of where its skin had split.

It's mortal. Sophie wanted to scream the phrase but was too breathless to make a sound. *It no longer has a vessel, and that means it can be killed!*

The Grimlock's maw widened horrifically, showing rows of long, viciously sharp teeth, and its eyes smoldered. Sophie caught a glimpse of a dark shape looming behind the Grimlock, but then her attention was dragged back to her own situation as Rose's boot connected with her ribs. She cried out and hunched over, tears blurring her vision, knowing that she had to fight back but unable to breathe.

A deep, bellowing roar shook the room, rattling the window-panes and making Sophie flinch. The Grimlock stepped away from Joseph as Garrett, blood running over one side of his face and his eyes filled with mad fury, swiped at the creature with the fireplace's poker.

Rose looked toward her master. The second of distraction was the chance Sophie had needed, and she kicked at the other woman's legs, knocking them out from under her. Rose collapsed to the ground and twisted, her spine rotating unnaturally as she turned. Sophie crawled toward the table, stretched a hand out to feel along its surface, and caught the knife in the same instant that Rose's cold, bony hands fixed around her ankle and dragged her backward.

"You dare defy my master?" Rose hissed, digging her nails into Sophie's skin until the pain was excruciating. "You think you can alter your fate, stupid child?"

Sophie slashed the knife toward the cadaver's face. It cut through the veil, shredding it, and impaled the area over Rose's left eye. The woman howled as a thick black substance, much like the Grimlock's blood, spurted out of the cut.

Instead of retreating as Sophie had hoped, Rose lurched forward. "Fool!" she screeched and clawed at Sophie's hands and face. Sophie jerked back to avoid the nails as Rose pinned her to the ground.

Suddenly, the black-eyed woman jerked back. Sophie dared to lower her arms and saw a second black-clothed figure behind Rose. One skeletal hand was snagged in Rose's hair and the other fixed around her throat as she pulled Sophie's attacker away.

The painting above the fireplace was empty. *Miss Bishop.*

The two women made a striking comparison. Both wore black dresses and had immaculate posture, but while Rose had a primal, bestial energy, Miss Bishop radiated righteous anger as she slammed Rose's head against the wall. There was a sickening crunch as Rose's skull fractured. Rose stretched her bony fingers forward, clawing at Miss Bishop's face, but Miss Bishop was already long dead, and the cuts were no impediment. She maintained her grip on Rose's hair and threw the corpse into the wall again, and again, and again, until Rose's one remaining eye rolled back in her skull, and her twitching hands fell still.

Miss Bishop didn't linger but swirled toward the Grimlock. It and Garrett circled each other, both defensive, both bleeding. Even as Miss Bishop rushed forward, Garrett swiped the poker toward the Grimlock. The beast dodged the blow then darted closer. It slammed into Garrett and forced him into the wall with a sickening crack.

Sophie didn't watch any further. She blinked blood out of her eyes and crawled toward the man who lay on the ground. Her heart froze at what she saw.

Joseph was on his back, eyes opened but cloudy. His breaths came in quick, thin gasps as the red stain underneath him grew larger with every heartbeat.

"Joseph." Sophie bent close, her hand hovering over his cheek. His eyes flicked toward her, and recognition chased the fog away.

"Get out," he rasped. "You have to get out."

The fear, previously held at bay by adrenaline, reared its ugly head. A need to scream choked her. She pressed her forehead to Joseph's and kissed his white cheek. She could feel him fading in her arms. *Not now... I can't lose him now...*

Sophie looked up, desperate for any kind of help. Garrett had dropped his poker and was clutching his right arm. Sophie thought it might be broken. The Grimlock was backed into a corner and snarling as Miss Bishop advanced on it. Every time it lunged at her, Miss Bishop disappeared like a wisp of smoke chased away by a breeze and reappeared behind him to deliver a fresh blow. She was faster than the heavy monster could match, and she slashed at its hide with the knife Sophie had dropped.

Sophie looked back at Joseph. His eyes had fallen closed. "Help," she gasped. "He needs help—"

He can't die now. Not after we found cessant's bloom—

Sophie gasped and turned to look for the cup. It was still lying beside the chaise longue but had been knocked over during the fight. Sophie ran for it. The path took her dangerously close to the Grimlock's corner, and she could sense its furious lamp eyes following her and feel its bellow rattle through her bones. She didn't spare it any attention but snatched up the cup and looked inside. A tiny amount of turquoise liquid clung to its base.

She was back at Joseph's side in a heartbeat, and she tipped the cup over his parted lips. Four drops fell, and she hit the cup's base to chase out an extra two. She threw the cup aside and held her breath as she watched his face. His eyes were still open, but they were unfocussed, and he didn't seem to be breathing any longer.

A tearing noise pulled Sophie's attention from her husband. She saw Miss Bishop collapse to the floor in a billow of black silk as she failed to disappear in time to avoid the beast's claws. The Grimlock drew itself to its full height, its blood-soaked head grazing the ceiling, and latched its attention onto Sophie and Joseph.

It's starved for energy, she realized. *It needs to eat if it wants to win this battle—and we're the easiest targets.*

She could see its muscles tense in preparation for the attack. She hunched over Joseph, shielding him, her breath frozen in her lungs and her heart pounding like a drum.

The Grimlock leaped toward them with the fluidity and enormous power of a great cat. Its maw gaped open, and the furious, white-glowing eyes locked onto Sophie's face.

It never hit.

A small figure moved between them at the last second, raised Garrett's poker, and aimed it at the beast's chest. The Grimlock was airborne and charging with an immense amount of momentum, and it had no chance of stopping. A sickening crunch echoed through the room as it impaled itself on the iron pole.

Elise's expression held none of the wild anger of her father's, only a deep, pervasive loathing. Her mouth was drawn into a tight line, and her eyes blazed with quiet, satisfied purpose. She was tiny compared to the Grimlock but didn't so much as flinch as the beast collapsed on top of her.

They both crumpled to the floor, but the Grimlock did not stay down. It howled as it threw itself back and contorted, trying to escape the metal that entered through its chest and extended out of its back. It writhed, twisted, turned, and stumbled.

Elise sat up carefully. A smile—the first genuine smile Sophie had seen her give—crossed the girl's face as she watched the monster.

The Grimlock staggered, one claw-tipped hand clutching the site where the pole entered its chest, and its black eyes darted over the room's occupants. Rose, her skull cracked down its center, lay in a heap on the floor. Garrett still held his broken arm, but the aggression painted on his face said he had no qualms about reentering the fight. Sophie crouched over Joseph's prone body, ready to defend her husband. Miss Bishop slowly rose from the ground, pulling herself to her full height, her eyes narrowed at the beast. And Elise smiled.

"*Ngh…*" The Grimlock tugged on the metal pole, but it was firmly lodged in its chest—piercing its heart. "No—"

"Yes," Elise said, and the Grimlock collapsed.

CHAPTER 30
DESOLATION

SOPHIE DIDN'T DARE TAKE her eyes from the fallen beast. Its torso was propped a few inches off the floor by the bar that ran through its chest, and thick, sludge-like blood slowly seeped from around the wound. When the Grimlock had been intangible, its heart had been whatever vessel it lived in—whether house or human. But its quest for freedom, for a physical form, had been its downfall; without an external heart to shield it, the Grimlock's coveted physical form had made its real, internal heart vulnerable.

"You're hurt."

The soft, beautifully familiar voice made Sophie jump. She looked at Joseph. His eyes had regained their alertness. He was soaked in drying blood—both the Grimlock's and his own—but his breathing was no longer ragged, and Sophie thought some color had returned to his cheeks. She didn't know whether she wanted to smile or cry as she stroked his wet hair away from his forehead with shaking fingers. "It w-worked."

Joseph sat up in a smooth motion, his eyebrows contracting as he scanned Sophie's face. The scratches on her cheeks burned, and she felt a bruise forming on her jaw. "Damn it, I should never have let you come here."

"It was worth it." Sophie didn't want to take her eyes away from Joseph's face, but she nodded at the Grimlock. "We're free."

The storm clouds that had plagued their stay at Kensington had been evaporating since the Grimlock's death. Sunlight streamed through the window and painted a large patch of golden light on the carpet. In the center of that glowing square lay the Grimlock. Small tendrils of black smoke leaked from the beast's open mouth, eyes, and wound. They drifted about the body, catching the light for a brief moment before disappearing.

Joseph watched the monster for a moment, then his attention shifted to his family. "Elise, are you hurt?"

The girl stood just outside the square of light, hands clasped in front, and smiled down at the creature. She gave the impression of an innocent child who had stumbled on a curiosity. Only the glitter in her black eyes hinted at her delight. "No."

"Garrett. How bad is it?"

"Pah. I'll live." Garrett was pale, clutching his arm and leaning against the wall, but his mustache bristled. "And you?"

"Good. No, better than that—" Joseph paused to take a deep breath then smiled at Sophie as he exhaled. "The scars' tightness is gone. It seems you'll have to live with me a little longer, my dear."

The days of fear drained out of Sophie. She rocked forward, not caring that he was soaked in blood, and rested her forehead in the nook under Joseph's chin. She dug her fingers into his shirt and held him close, afraid to let him go and unable to stop smiling.

"Shh, it's all right, my darling." He wrapped one arm about her shoulders and stroked her hair. "Let's move you to somewhere you can rest. The library perhaps."

Sophie tried to shake her head. "You shouldn't move too much—the monster hurt you—"

"*I'm* fine. *You* need rest. And new clothes. And a bath." He began to laugh. "And your life returned to normal if we can manage it."

She chuckled against his warm skin. "I have everything I need right here."

The gentle rhythm of his hand brushing over her hair was hypnotic. The aches, fear, and adrenaline began to melt away, and tiredness crept in to take its place. Sophie couldn't do any more than sigh at the sound of Joseph's voice in her ear. "Everything is all right now. Relax, my darling. My brave, sweet, clever darling."

For the first time since visiting Kensington, Sophie's dreams weren't troubled. She was vaguely aware of voices talking and blankets being tucked around her, but they didn't disturb her. When she woke, she couldn't tell how long she'd been asleep except that daylight had changed to night. A bright fire and multiple candles lit the room, but it still took Sophie a few minutes to identify the tall, dark shapes as bookshelves.

"Forgive me for disturbing you." Joseph spoke quietly and

stroked her hair back from her forehead. "I would have let you sleep longer, but I didn't want to make you wait for this."

Sophie tried to sit up and grimaced. The day's strained muscles, scrapes, and bruises protested against the motion, and she closed her eyes and breathed deeply until she regained control.

Joseph held an arm behind her back to brace her. "We have more of the flower. It has not long finished boiling and should be cool enough to drink."

Sophie blinked at the cup Joseph offered her. It held the same gray-blue syrup they'd given to Elise the night before. "What—where did you get it?"

"From the chasm." Joseph smiled at Sophie's shocked expression. "Don't look so anxious, my darling. I was significantly more prepared than you were; I used a rope tethered to a tree and had Elise as my lookout."

"Were you troubled by any of the dead?"

"No, thankfully." He pressed a kiss to her forehead. "They seem to have disappeared with the Grimlock's death. But the river is engorged, even more than yesterday, and has washed away almost all vegetation. It took me more than an hour to find what I did, and even that was only three plants."

He nodded over his shoulder, and Sophie shifted forward to see two saucepans sitting on the reading desk. They were filled with muddy soil, and each held a tiny, battered, blue-flowered plant. "One to make the brew for Garrett and you and two to keep, provided they survive. Come, I hate seeing you in pain. Drink."

The liquid was bitter and still hot. Sophie tried not to choke as she swallowed it.

"Is it that bad?" Joseph's smile was apologetic. "I don't remember much from last night, let alone how the drink tasted. Garrett told me what happened, though. He said you were fantastic."

Joseph shifted to sit beside Sophie and looped his arm around her shoulders. She leaned her head against his chest and closed her eyes as an incredible heat bloomed outward from her stomach. It felt like liquid fire coursing through her veins and sent strange prickles across her skin.

"Remarkable," Joseph murmured. Sophie followed his gaze to a scab on her arm. The dried blood remained, but the skin underneath knitted itself back together. She inhaled deeply and realized the ribs Rose had kicked were no longer sore. The aches and tiredness seemed to slough away, shedding from her like dead skin peeling off.

As the pain disappeared, she began to pay more attention to her surroundings. Faint snoring came from the other side of the room, where she could see a large figure—Garrett—sleeping propped against a shelf. Elise, wrapped in blankets, slept at his side. The room was warm, thanks to the fire, and moonlight streamed through the windows. Sophie turned her attention back to Joseph and examined him in the subdued lighting.

He'd washed the blood off and changed into clean clothes. His black hair was swept away from his face, and though he was still gaunter than she would have liked, his aspect had lost the frightening ashen pallor, and his eyes were no longer circled by shadows.

"You're well?" she asked.

"Better than I could have hoped." He undid the top button of his shirt and pulled the fabric aside. "The scars remain but have reduced to just surface marks."

Sophie brushed her fingers over the streak of white that ran over his muscles. The scars had faded but still stood out clearly against his skin. *As long as they're not hurting him.*

She glanced back at herself, felt her face heat from embarrassment, and tugged the blanket up to preserve her modesty. Joseph had washed her face and arms, but she still wore the mud-caked, bloodied chemise and could feel that her hair was a mat of dirty tangles. She looked up at Joseph to apologize but fell silent at his expression.

"You're gorgeous," he said, adoration shining in his eyes. He tilted forward to steal a kiss, and Sophie didn't have the self-control to resist. He brushed his lips across hers, teasing, before capturing her mouth. She sighed against him then trembled as his fingers explored the sensitive skin around her neck. "Gorgeous," he mumbled between kisses.

She would have been glad to spend the rest of the night with him like that, kissing him and feeling his heart beat under her fingers, but they were eventually shaken apart by a particularly loud snore from Garrett. Joseph laughed and gave her cheek a final caress. "I had better give him the tea for his arm," he said, standing reluctantly. "Then we can boil some water and clear away the dirt if you like."

They had no bathtub, but Joseph heated enough water in pails that it wasn't too difficult to wash. After she'd scrubbed herself and changed into a mercifully clean dress, Joseph had her sit in the stone hallway so he could wash and untangle her hair.

While he worked at the knots and poured water over her curls, they talked with an honesty they'd never shared before. Sophie learned that her husband did prefer the country but that he wasn't averse to living in the city if she wanted to be near her father. He liked dogs, hunting, and sport fishing. He'd never grieved for Rose.

"Living in Northwood, we were all familiar with the concept that our lives could end at any moment," he said, running his fingers through her now-clean hair and combing out any tangles that he found. "Rose and I were never close. We tolerated each other—were cordial even—but I always preferred Garrett's company."

Once he was satisfied with her hair, he took her back to the library and set her by the fire to dry it. By the time Joseph had finished braiding her hair and Sophie turned around to meet his smile, he no longer felt like a stranger.

He was her Joseph. Kind. Patient. Intelligent. And very dearly loved.

CHAPTER 31
TWO FUNERALS

THAT NIGHT, JOSEPH AND Sophie shared a bundle of blankets in the library. They tangled together, limbs wrapped around each other, and as she drifted into sleep, Sophie thought she would be happy to stay there all of the following day until the coach came to retrieve them.

The morning brought a swath of work, though, and there were decisions that needed to be agreed on. They made their first task retrieving Miss Bishop's remains from the collapsed section of the house. They dug her grave in the space beside her partner's and dragged in a fresh rock to act as her headstone. They took a lot of care with the funeral; Miss Bishop had saved their lives, and Sophie knew she would never forget the good that the woman had done for them. As they concluded the prayers and Sophie raised her head, she caught a glimpse of a dark figure in the woods behind the graves. *Thank you,* she mouthed and could have sworn the figure gave a brief nod before vanishing into the shadows.

When they returned to the house, they had to decide what to do with the two bodies that still lay in the parlor. The Grimlock looked strangely collapsed, as though part of its mass had bled out with the black smoke that had flowed from its mouth and wound. At the other side of the room, Rose lay crumpled against the wall, her eyes wide and sightless and her papery skin split where her skull had cracked.

"We should bury her," Joseph said quietly. "For what she once was if nothing else."

"Agreed." Garrett went to collect a blanket to wrap her in.

They didn't place Rose in the same area as Miss Bishop and Mr. Trent but dug her grave in a shady area near the collapsed section of the house. It was peaceful and relatively green there, and the funeral was respectful but brief.

Deciding what to do with the Grimlock was a much harder choice. None of them were eager to touch its shiny black hide, and it was far too large for one person to move. Eventually, Elise suggested the solution. "Leave it here," she said, eyeing the black monster with mixed revulsion and triumph. "Let it stay under Miss Bishop's painting. She spent her life trying to destroy it, didn't she? Leave it here, unburied, so that her painting can watch over her victory for eternity."

That's strangely fitting, Sophie thought, looking up at the large oil painting over the mantel. *Miss Bishop's spirit may have moved on, but her memory can stand guard over the Grimlock's bones.*

The portrait, haughty and proud, gazed out at the room. Sophie had to smile at the sight. Having met the real Miss Bishop, she knew the artist had injected his own presuppositions into the image. The true Miss Bishop held none of the disdain that her portrait did. She had been strong, courageous, and dedicated and was a woman Sophie was proud to have known, if only briefly.

None of them were sad to leave Kensington the following morning. Elise, reveling in her freedom, ran backward and forward through the field that separated the house from the woods. Joseph and Garrett followed, each carrying a small case, while Sophie held the two pots with the remaining cessant's blooms. Garrett had brought a vast supply of equipment for the stay, but they would be taking almost none of it on their trip back—only a handful of family heirlooms, the most important books from Miss Bishop's library, a change of clothes for each of them, some food, and the two remaining flowers. Everything else was considered replaceable and left to grace Kensington's halls until the building collapsed into the dirt.

Sophie had been worried about crossing the chasm now that the bridge lay useless, but the solution turned out to be remarkably simple. Joseph and Garret spent an hour cutting down one of the vast trees, aiming it so that it fell across the gorge. The trunk was wide and surprisingly stable, but Joseph crossed at the same time as Sophie, his hand held toward her for the entire journey in case she needed support.

She no longer found the drop frightening, though. As they shimmied along the bark and toward the boughs that rested on the opposite clearing, she peeked over the edge and was able to smile at the rushing water that filled the gorge's base. She'd stood on that ground, and somehow, that had removed its power over her.

They picnicked in the clearing. Elise dashed through the forest, repeatedly weaving among the trees until Garrett, ever the anxious parent, called her back. Then she would return for a bite of food before racing off again. Sophie couldn't keep from laughing at the girl's antics. Only a few days ago, she'd grieved because Elise might never be able to experience her coming out into society. Now she wondered if such a feat would be possible without the energetic, opinionated, unexpectedly stubborn girl causing a dozen scandals.

The sun had started to dip by the time they heard the clatter of hooves coming from the woods. Joseph's coach appeared, and the footman, although surprised to see the fallen tree blocking his road, helped load their small amount of luggage. They carried the plants in their laps to prevent them from being crushed. It had been agreed that Joseph and Sophie would keep one of the plants and Garrett and Elise would have the second.

As the coach turned and began retracing its path into the woods, Sophie rested her head against Joseph's shoulder. He murmured happily as he leaned close to kiss her hair.

CHAPTER 32
HOME

Three Months Later

"STILL WORKING, MY DEAR?"

Sophie startled then laughed as she turned to face Joseph. "You can't sneak up on me like that. I'll spill my ink."

He stood in her study's doorway, a striking figure in his evening dress, and grinned at her. "You look magnificent."

She rose and crossed to him. "Do you think it's too much? It won't be a large party—"

He caught her hand, pulled her against him, and kissed her before she could finish. His hands tangled in her hair, simultaneously gentle and heated as he pressed them together. He sighed when they finally pulled apart. "You don't know what you do to me, my darling."

And you don't know what you do to me. Sophie laughed as she pressed her pink face against his chest.

Joseph planted small kisses across the parts of her cheek and neck he could reach. "As much as I would like to prolong this, our coach is waiting, and people will talk if we don't make an appearance."

"Oh—I didn't realize it was so late—one moment—"

Sophie ducked out of Joseph's arms and ran back to her writing desk. Joseph followed and looked over her shoulder as she cleaned her pen and fixed the lid back onto the pot of ink. "How is it coming?"

"Very well. I shouldn't have been writing tonight, I know. I'll get ink all over this"—Sophie waved a hand at her dress, a floaty, gauzy blue affair with ruffles around the skirts—"if I'm not careful, but I thought of something else that I wanted to note down before I forgot."

Joseph looked at the pile of completed pages stacked neatly on one side of the desk. "Better to write it down while the memory's still fresh."

The book had started as a minor hobby, but as the stack of papers grew, Sophie had become increasingly excited about it. Joseph said he would help her publish it when it was ready and promised her a handsome leather binding and thick, rich paper.

Her study was in their house's corner room, next to their bedroom and overlooking the flower gardens that flourished outside. On the corner desk, carefully kept in the indirect light it preferred, was a cessant's bloom. It had been planted in a pretty blue pot and looked no different from the other indoors plants dotting their home. They kept two of its brothers in their city house.

"You're spoiling me," Sophie had accused Joseph when he first suggested two houses, but he had only laughed.

"Perhaps I am. But there are very few things I enjoy more. Besides, this way we will have a house in the country for when we want peace and a house in the city for when the country becomes too dull."

They were staying in the country that month and had been fortunate enough to fall in with a friendly group who had invited them to a party that night. The sun had not long set, and Sophie could see the faint glow of the carriage's lantern outside her window.

"We'd better go," Sophie murmured, leaning back against Joseph to enjoy the solid warmth he offered.

"Yes, we'd better." He wrapped his arms around her waist and nuzzled her neck. "In an hour or two."

Sophie laughed, spun out of his hold, took his hand, and raced to the door with him. "Come on, or we'll never leave."

The study fell silent as the couple left, ran down the stairs, collected their coats from the butler, and disappeared into the night. The papers, arranged neatly on the table and covered in dry ink, waited for their mistress to return and resume the half-finished passage. The title on the first page of the completed stack shimmered in the moonlight. *Grimlock: The Beast with a Thousand Hearts.*

ABOUT THE AUTHOR

Darcy Coates is the *USA Today* bestselling author of *Hunted*, *The Haunting of Ashburn House*, *Craven Manor*, and more than a dozen other horror and suspense titles. She lives on the Central Coast of Australia with her family, cats, and a garden full of herbs and vegetables. Darcy loves forests, especially old-growth forests where the trees dwarf anyone who steps between them. Wherever she lives, she tries to have a mountain range close by.

VOICES IN THE SNOW

NO ONE ESCAPES THE STILLNESS.

Clare remembers the cold. She remembers dark shapes in the snow and a terror she can't explain. And then…nothing. When she wakes in a stranger's home, he tells her she was in an accident. Clare wants to leave, but a vicious snowstorm has blanketed the world in white, and there's nothing she can do but wait.

They should be alone, but Clare's convinced something else is creeping about the surrounding woods, watching. Waiting. Between the claustrophobic storm and the inescapable sense of being hunted, Clare is on edge…and increasingly certain of one thing: her car crash wasn't an accident. Something is waiting for her to step outside the fragile safety of the house…something monstrous, something unfeeling. Something desperately hungry.

THE HAUNTING OF ASHBURN HOUSE

THERE'S SOMETHING WRONG WITH ASHBURN HOUSE...

Everyone knows about Ashburn House. They whisper its old owner went mad, and restless ghosts still walk the halls. But when Adrienne inherits the crumbling old mansion, she only sees it as a lifeline...until darkness falls.

As the nights grow ever more restless, it becomes clear something twisted lives in Adrienne's house. Chasing the threads of a decades-old mystery, it isn't long before she realizes she's become prey to something deeply unnatural and intensely resentful. She has no idea how to escape. She has no idea how to survive. Only one thing is certain: Ashburn's dead are not at rest.

THE HAUNTING OF
BLACKWOOD HOUSE

HOW LONG COULD YOU SURVIVE?

As the daughter of spiritualists, Mara's childhood was filled with séances and scam mediums. Now she's ready to start over with her fiancé, Neil, far away from the superstitions she's learned to loathe…but her past isn't willing to let her go so easily. And neither is Blackwood House.

When Mara and Neil purchased the derelict property, they were warned that ever since the murder of its original owner, things have changed. Strange shadows stalk the halls. Doors creak open by themselves. Voices whisper in the night. And watchful eyes follow her every move. But Mara's convinced she can't possibly be in danger. Because ghosts aren't real…are they?

THE HOUSE NEXT DOOR

NO ONE STAYS HERE FOR LONG.

Josephine began to suspect something was wrong with the house next door when its family fled in the middle of the night, the children screaming, the mother crying. They never came back. No family stays at Marwick House for long. No life lingers beyond its blackened windows. No voices drift from its ancient halls. Once, Josephine swore she saw a woman's silhouette pacing through the upstairs room…but that's impossible. No one had been there in a long, long time.

But now someone new has moved next door, and Marwick House is slowly waking up. Torn between staying away and warning the new tenant, Josephine only knows that if she isn't careful, she may be its next victim…

THE FOLCROFT GHOSTS

EVERY FAMILY HAS ITS SECRETS.

When their mother is hospitalized, Tara and Kyle are sent to stay with their only remaining relatives. Their elderly grandparents seem friendly at first, and the rambling house is full of fun nooks and crannies to explore. But strange things keep happening. Something is being hidden away, kept safely out of sight...and the children can't shake the feeling that it's watching them.

When a violent storm cuts off their only contact with the outside world, Tara and Kyle must find a way to protect themselves from their increasingly erratic grandparents...and from the ghosts that haunt the Folcrofts' house. But can they ever hope to escape the unforgivable secret that has ensnared their family for generations?

For more info about Sourcebooks's books and authors, visit:
sourcebooks.com

THE CARROW HAUNT

THE DEAD ARE RESTLESS HERE.

Remy is a tour guide for the notoriously haunted Carrow House. When she's asked to host guests researching Carrow's phenomena, she hopes to finally experience some of the sightings that made the house famous.

At first, it's everything they hoped for. Then a storm moves in, cutting off their contact with the outside world, and things quickly take a sinister turn. But it isn't until one of the guests dies under strange circumstances that Remy is forced to consider the possibility that the ghost of the house's original owner—a twisted serial killer—still walks the halls. And by then it's too late to escape…